Walking

with the

Fishermen

C. S. Clifford

First published in Great Britain by C. S. Clifford

ISBN: 978-0993-1-9572-3

Printed and bound in the UK

A catalogue record of this book is available from the British Library

Edited by Jo Clifford and Claire Spinks

Cover artwork and design by Claire Spinks

www.csclifford.co.uk

For the children I've taught who told me they didn't believe.

What if you are wrong?

To Charlie

Best Wishes

CSC

Prologue

Matt and James discovered a portal to another time and place at the start of their summer holidays, by chance, during their training to get fit for the approaching rugby season. While swimming underwater in the local river, Matt had found a cave at the base of a waterfall. The two boys eagerly explored the cavern and tunnel leading from it to a second waterfall. Running alongside was a narrow ledge which allowed them to pass through the deluge into a strange new world.

This is their third adventure through the waterfall and into the unknown...

A Strange New World

Matt stood beneath the full force of the water, leaving only his head clear of the deluge.

"Wow! It's a lot more powerful than last time. There's far more water falling, watch your footing," he shouted to his friend, patiently waiting his turn.

James nodded, not even attempting a verbal answer; competing against the thundering echo of water in the enclosed space of the cave seemed pointless. He watched carefully as Matt edged on to the start of the ledge that would lead to another time and place. Once Matt's head and body had disappeared into the waterfall, he took a few deep breaths, then followed slowly into the torrent. As his head was engulfed in the cold water, he sidled to the left, using his toes to feel the way along the ledge that was just wide enough for his feet. Situated just a few centimetres above the floor of the cave, it was wet and slippery, but it led the only way through and beyond the waterfall. James held his breath as he made his way slowly through the tumultuous flow. Matt was right, the volume of water was definitely greater than they had experienced before. He remembered clearly how much weaker the force of the water had felt then, as well as the lower noise levels. In fact, thinking about it now, these had been different on each occasion they had passed through the drenching time portal. He wondered if it signified anything.

As he emerged foot first, quickly followed by his torso and head, James exhaled with relief, shaking his head to expel the liquid streaming from his body. It didn't matter how many times he did this, the relief at passing through was always intense as he resurfaced from the isolation of the water. He took a large gulp of air, immediately noticing its warmth as he breathed in. Continuing sideways, hugging the rock face until the ledge petered out, he stepped onto a large rock, making his way over several others that led down to the ground. As usual, the waterfall flowed into a small pool that disappeared swiftly into the ground with barely a trace.

Matt stood there, grinning at him.

"Get a load of this place!" He thumped James on the back excitedly.

James looked around eagerly, drinking in the unfamiliar scenery.

"We must be somewhere completely different for a change – I've never seen anywhere like this in England!" he said incredulously, eying crumbling rocks and rough, sandy ground, desiccated-looking shrubs scattered thinly into the distance.

"If it wasn't for the shrubs, I'd swear we'd ended up on the moon! We have to be pretty high up for the plants to look like this."

James laughed and started to look more closely.

"You're right, but finding a way down isn't going to be easy. I think we're somewhere Mediterranean, maybe Greece or Turkey, somewhere like that. The dryness and colour of the ground look like photographs in holiday brochures."

"Abroad makes a bit of a change, but I don't really mind where the time portal has taken us – we know it'll lead to new friends and adventures. Come on – let's try and find a way down to civilisation!"

James grinned at his friend's impatient nature and his love for the adrenaline rush that accompanied it. Although he knew how this felt, he preferred to stop and think a little before blindly rushing in.

Matt hadn't waited for a reply. He'd simply picked a direction that took his liking and strode off. It took just a few paces for James to catch up, his longer and leaner frame eating up the distance faster than his shorter, stockier friend. Both teenagers had mature attitudes for their ages but still retained their boyish enthusiasm for excitement and adventure. The pair had different strengths and weaknesses that balanced their friendship, with James' calm maturity offsetting Matt's headstrong impetuousness.

They both shared a passion for playing rugby and were at their peak in terms of physical fitness. They loved being part of a team and getting things done, but they also relished being part of their own smaller unit and were virtually inseparable both at school and home.

"What do you think about the waterfall being fuller than before?" Matt asked his friend. "It's not like we've had massive rainstorms recently."

"I noticed it when we came through last time as well – it was lighter than the first time. Perhaps it gets more powerful the further back in time we go?"

"I hadn't thought about it like that but, if it's true, then we must have travelled way back because the water was a *lot* stronger than before."

James didn't answer, keeping further thoughts to himself until he had something tangible to go on. Instead, he pointed the way forward, where the terrain started to fall away at an angle. Something told him that the descent they had to make might not be quite as straightforward as he had hoped.

As they came to the edge of the incline, the drop revealed the great height they stood at, overlooking a massive expanse of land below. In the distance, the shimmering ocean seemed to border it for as far as they could see.

"Look at that. James! You don't see views like that very often."

James whistled in awe as he studied the scene below.

Great swathes of green covered the fertile land several hundred feet below them and he thought he could make out some sections that were being farmed. He couldn't see livestock of any kind, but that was not particularly surprising given their current height.

The sea was azure-blue reflecting the brilliance of the cerulean sky, and the blazing sun made it sparkle like a million densely packed stars on a clear night.

At the water's edge was a line of tiny, dark shapes and, although ill-defined, James thought he could just make out boats of some sort. Behind them were some barely visible structures, the same colour as the dusty earth surrounding them; their grouping suggesting they might be houses.

"We're going to have to be careful going down there, it's really steep. And I don't like the look of that surface too much either. It's so loose, it's going to be treacherous underfoot," said Matt breaking his friend's silent study of the landscape.

"It does look dangerous, but I saw a survival guy negotiate slopes like this once. As he went down, he kept really low to the ground, so that if he felt himself slipping he could immediately sit down and use his feet as brakes."

"Sounds like fun! The slope's only about a hundred metres down – do you fancy turning this into a bit of a challenge?"

James shook his head briefly.

"No, not this time. We're far too likely to injure ourselves and we don't know what's in store for us yet."

Matt's face fell, though even he could see that James was probably right. His brief flirtation with common sense lasted barely a moment, however.

"I'll go first," he said with a sudden grin, and was off before James had time to answer.

Unfortunately, following immediately behind Matt was not the best idea, as the cloud of dust he created caked and choked James, who arrived coughing violently at the bottom of the slope.

Matt offered a hand to help him up from his sprawled position, slapping him half-heartedly several times on the back. Whether this was to assist with his coughing fit or to remove some of the dust covering him wasn't that obvious to James who finished choking and spluttered a request to look out for a stream before proceeding to spit out some of the dust.

"Yeah, yeah," said Matt, disinterestedly. "Look there's a track over there. It definitely looks firmer than the stuff we've just come down."

For the next half hour, they followed the track as it wound its way down between the rocky foothills. As they descended, the dust gave way to occasional pockets of soil; small alpine-like flowers adding tiny specks of colour to the otherwise lifeless shades of beige surrounding them. Shrubs gave way to bushes, and bushes, in turn, to trees. From among them came the sound of a small stream bursting from an underground spring.

They left the path with hastened steps to quench their thirst that had intensified with the rise in temperature.

"Cor, I needed that! I thought my tongue was going to be permanently stuck to the roof of my mouth," said James with a relieved look on his face.

"Mine too. Shh, can you hear that?"

"What?"

Matt paused to listen before answering. "I thought I heard rustling in the trees down there."

"Probably an animal."

Matt shrugged before heading back to the path and continuing the descent. They hadn't taken many more steps before they heard a shout and the sound of a stick hitting something repeatedly. Stopping abruptly, Matt darted into the trees with James on his heels.

"What did you come in here for?" asked James, slightly taken aback.

"Not sure, but I just got a gut feeling that now's not a good time to reveal ourselves. I thought we should watch and see who comes past."

James nodded, surprised by his friend's uncharacteristic restraint. After a few seconds of silence, the beating started again, immediately followed by loud voices.

The boys crouched behind a large bush bearing needle-like thorns that threatened to tear the flesh from their bodies, and focussed on the direction of the sounds. A minute passed before a procession of goats started to appear, walking languidly up the mountain. Behind them came two young boys, dressed in loincloths, beating sticks on an object they both carried, making a dull metallic sound.

And behind them marched three Roman soldiers, dressed in outfits similar to the ones Matt and James had worn when they were forced to take part in a performance of *Anthony and Cleopatra* at school. The leading soldier had a whip in his hand and was using it to 'encourage' the boys to move faster. The whip cracked to the side of the two boys repeatedly and the man occasionally allowed the tip to graze the boys' olive-coloured skin. Each connecting strike brought a squeal from one of them and left a small red mark.

"I think we've definitely come a long way back in time, Matt. Did you see what they were wearing?"

"The one in front, the one with the whip, was a Decanus – it's why he had a finer uniform. The history books have at least got the clothing right! So, Roman soldiers means we could be in Italy."

"I s'pose so, but the Roman Empire spread out all over the world at the height of their reign, so we could be anywhere. A Decanus is a leader of ten men and he only had two with him. I wonder what happened to the rest."

"Could be that they split up for a different task I guess, which means they might be somewhere around here too. I got a weird feeling as they passed by, something gnawed at me not to trust them, some instinct or something."

"No doubt we're already in the guise of somebody else so there's no telling how much of what we're feeling is ourselves or something to do with the characters we've become. But let's follow your instincts and wait a while before we carry on."

"Sounds like a plan to me," said Matt, nodding seriously.

"I didn't like the way that Decanus was using a whip on those boys, they were already doing what they were told. He seemed to be enjoying inflicting pain on them."

"I didn't like that either, but we can't judge them on the way things first appear to us. This is a very different time and a place... I hope we don't see him again, though."

Simon

James waited for Matt to decide when to move. He hadn't experienced the uncomfortable feelings that Matt had but respected his friend's instincts as much as he did his own. Sometimes you had to go with your gut, even when there seemed no rhyme or reason for it.

The wait seemed to last longer than the five minutes it actually was before Matt rose from the bush and headed back onto the path. They continued down the trail, at times so steep that rough steps had been hewn into the hillside. Eventually, it petered out onto grassy pasture which unfurled lazily before them. From the air, they would have seen that it rolled on for miles to the left and right of their position like the coiling body of a snake, but, directly in front of them, it seemed to stretch just a few hundred metres. As they walked, the ground under their feet became softer and spongey and treading on the clumps of the thickening grass gave them a spring in their step.

"How far do you think we've walked now, James?" asked Matt. "We must have been at it for a couple of hours."

"Five or six miles I suspect. Normally, we'd have covered more in the same time, but that track was a bit rough, to say the least."

"I wonder how much further we have to go. I'm starting to get hungry. We should've brought sandwiches with us."

"You're always hungry! I'm not sure how far we have to go, but the slope's not quite so steep here. Hopefully, we'll be able to see that stretch of land next to the sea when we've crossed this grass."

James was right. At the end of the pasture, the hillside dropped away steeply to a series of cliffs that revealed the final leg of their descent. The view here was almost as stunning as it had been higher up; the sea dominated the scene, with the sun still reflecting brightly upon it but from a lower angle in the sky, swathing a line of gold across from the shore to the horizon.

From here they could easily make out the line of boats they thought they'd seen from the top, although these were of a strange and crude design, quite different from what they'd expected.

Tracing their eyes back towards their current position, they could see the buildings more clearly too. Still too far to see what they were made of for certain, Matt suggested they were part stone, part earth judging by their predominantly bleached sandy colour. It was clearly a village, though its size could only be guessed at from here as the buildings extended beneath the next incline.

Goats and chickens wandered through the settlement, presumably looking for food, letting out an occasional bleat or squawk if disturbed from their occupation. But the boys' attention was drawn mostly to the people milling around the buildings. Both men and women were dressed in long robes that concealed their entire bodies. They couldn't see if the head coverings were part of the robes or not, but they did suggest where in the world they might be.

"They look like Arabs. I think we were a bit off with this being Turkey or Greece. I reckon we're in the Middle East – Iran, Iraq, Jordan, Saudi Arabia – somewhere like that. If we've gone back in time as far as I think, then these places would have different names too," James said, thoughtfully.

"I don't know much about this part of the world or its history," replied Matt, shrugging his shoulders.

"Me neither, but that just makes it more interesting," James answered with a broad smile. "You know we could end up seeing more of the world than your average sailor at this rate!"

"I'm up for that, especially if we don't quite make the grade as international rugby stars of the future."

"I can't see much of a path down from here, so we can probably just go either way. What do you think?" asked Matt, before immediately moving off to his left.

James just laughed and followed him. It was so typical of Matt to decide for them.

The pasture at the edge of the grassland became crushed and damaged as the end of a path materialised beneath their feet. Following it, they started to descend once more. As the path widened, there was evidence of animals passing along it, and James knew that this had to be the main route down to the village which they had observed from higher up. Further down still, the grass disappeared altogether, to be replaced with sand that irritatingly entered their shoes as they inadvertently kicked it up with every step. Finally, the sandy slope levelled off and they walked towards a parade of boats and a few isolated figures working intently on their nets.

The water's edge was closer here than at the village, and it took only a few moments to reach the first of the boats. As they passed, a man working on the second in line called out to James in a hostile tone.

"Shalom, James. Why is it that you bring this man to our village? Has he not robbed us all of our money in the past?"

Before James could recover his composure from the strange greeting, a second figure appeared next to the first.

"Andrew! You know better than to speak in such a way," he said, calmly but no less forcibly.

"Sorry, Simon, but there will be trouble if that man goes into the village."

"Not if I have anything to do with it," replied the bigger man before walking towards James and Matt.

He stopped in front of James and clasped his forearm firmly.

"Shalom, James. It is good to see you again, my friend. How was your journey?"

"Shalom, Simon. It pleases me also to see you again," replied James, immediately improvising his response.

"Since you travel with this man, I assume he is as a friend to you, despite the fact that those around here see him as the opposite. It would be the courteous thing to introduce us."

"He has been my friend for a long time, Simon, and despite what the others think of him, will remain so. However, you have reminded me of my manners and for this I apologise. Simon, this is Matt. Matt – Simon."

Simon clasped Matt's forearm in the same manner as James.

"Shalom and welcome to our community. I'm sorry, what name did you give?"

Matt thought quickly. His name was a diminutive form based on the written word. Back in Roman times, few people would have been able to write, so his name would probably make no sense here.

He responded quickly, "Shalom, Simon. He has called me Matt since we were boys – my name is Matthew. I must thank you for not judging me as Andrew did."

"Do not worry about that now. I take it James, that you are on your way to your house to see your brother. If that is the case, then I am afraid that you will be disappointed, for he journeyed to Judaea some weeks ago and will not return for some time. I will walk with you, for your house will be dusty and have no fresh water. The blankets will need beating and it would be my pleasure to assist you for you must be tired after your journey."

"You are most kind, Simon. It is true that we have been travelling a long time and the terrain we have covered has not been easy."

The three of them walked at a casual pace towards the village and Matt noticed the contemptuous looks he received from several people. Did they all know him here? As they headed for one building in particular, facing the sea and boats, Simon paced ahead and opened the door for them. Matt and James stared at the building which was made of clay and stone with some parts of the walls built from clay bricks. The roof of the single-storey building was timber-framed and covered with clay.

Following Simon in to one central space, they saw two small-sized sleeping areas screened off on either side by a rough timber-frame and blankets. There was little else, apart from a small table with a crudely fashioned wooden bench on either side. An equally roughly made storage cupboard adorned the far wall, along with a couple of shelves.

Simon removed the shutters from the two windows to allow light to flood in, and the boys immediately saw how dirty the place really was. Simon grabbed a broom made from tightly packed twigs bound with twine to a sturdy branch, and began to sweep the floor, creating a fog of dust that quickly filled the small space. Stopping suddenly, he picked up two blankets from one of the makeshift beds and indicated for Matt to do the same.

"Take them outside and thrash them with the beater," he instructed, throwing it at Matt who caught it neatly as Simon recommenced sweeping.

Matt was only too happy to escape the thickening fog and James followed him outside, where they took turns to place a blanket over a length of strong twine tied between a pole and one of the roof rafters, and beat it mercilessly. Simon appeared, caked in dust but grinning widely, his teeth looking impossibly white under his fresh layer of grime. He had a leather bucket in each hand and strode off to the community well, where he filled them to overflowing and carried them back effortlessly.

"It would be my pleasure if you ate at my house tonight, my friends," he told them on his return.

"Your offer is very kind, Simon, but we are both exhausted and in need of some real sleep tonight," James replied, gratefully.

"In that case, allow me to bring you something instead, so that you do not have to tax yourself further."

"You are a good friend, Simon, and we will be pleased to accept your kind offer. We appreciate your understanding of our immediate needs," James told him.

Simon went back inside to continue sweeping, and clouds of dust were soon sent billowing through the open door and windows of the small building. Ten minutes later, Simon had completed the housework and came outside to join them. As he did so, a projectile thrown with some force hit Matt squarely on the biceps.

"What the heck?" he exclaimed, angrily.

"You must go inside," Simon told them and quickly ushered them in, protecting them from further attack.

"Enough of this!" Simon called out to the unseen attackers as he closed the door behind him.

"I am sorry that happened, Matthew, but it will take the people here some time to accept you as you are now, rather than as you used to be."

Matt didn't have a clue as to what Simon was talking about but nodded his acceptance of the apology nonetheless.

"I will call a meeting of the people tonight as you both sleep and talk to them about the way they are treating a visitor to our village and will ensure that this hostility ceases. I will go now and make the arrangements, but will return later with some food for you. For now, just rest and let sleep ease the suffering on your body the journey has caused."

With that, he turned and left before Matt or James could thank him.

"He seems like a decent sort of bloke," said James cheerfully.

"I, for one, am glad that he's around since I am clearly not too popular in these parts."

"Well, he seems to think he can sort it out – I guess we'll find out in the morning, but for now I want to see exactly what I look like."

"I don't see a pond anywhere to look at our reflection, and I'm pretty sure they didn't have mirrors during this period."

"Well, the rich probably had mirrors of polished gold, but I think they'll be a bit thin on the ground round here. However, Matt my friend, there are two buckets of freshly drawn water over there that will give us what we need."

They held their faces above the water, turning from side to side while staring at their reflections, before looking at each other and laughing in amusement.

Fishing for Food

"My beard is longer than yours," said Matt, instantly making a challenge out of nothing.

"That might be so, but just look at that nose of yours, not exactly straight is it?"

Both boys laughed and set about examining the contents of the room, few though there were. In fact, they were amazed at just how little there was: no spare clothing, only a single cooking vessel by the hearth of the fire, a few items and tools for mending nets and a small selection of blankets.

"Not exactly a lot for a couple of men our age, is there?" commented Matt ruefully.

"I s'pose the needs were pretty basic for this period, but I bet they have everything they need. They're clearly not wealthy, and fishing must be a hard life without modern conveniences – they don't even have a winch. How old do you think we are any way?"

"I'm guessing mid-twenties; it's hard to tell with the beards and long hair but somewhere round there."

"Perhaps we're not old enough to have acquired more than what's here."

"Yeah, and there's not much reward for such hard work. I bet we've been working since we were really young too, probably a family tradition."

"You're right, and there wouldn't have been any schools to

go to in this period of history, so boys would've helped in the family business."

Simon returned with a pot of stew some time later and some very unusual flat bread. He didn't stay long, knowing that the boys needed a good night's sleep.

"Do you need an early call, James? I assume that you're going out with the tide tomorrow?"

"Matthew and I will both be going out. He wants to see fishermen at work," answered James, quickly spotting the absence of his friend in the invitation. "What time is the tide? I've been away so long, I've lost track."

"An hour before sun up," Simon answered, before wishing them a good night and making his exit.

"It's a good job we have some experience around boats, 'cause I think we're going to need it. These boats have no engines and the sails don't exactly look in the best of condition," said Matt, recalling the last adventure they'd had through the time portal.

"Let's just take it one step at a time. At the moment, we don't even know which boat is ours," James said.

"That's easily sorted; if we arrive late, then whichever boat is unmanned must be ours."

"Just as long as we don't miss the tide. I have a feeling that we may well learn more about our purpose here if all goes well."

The two of them retired to their beds and slept surprisingly well.

They awoke while it was still dark but neither of them knew exactly how early it was. They had learnt on previous adventures that none of their modern gadgets worked once they'd gone through the time portal and hadn't even brought their mobiles with them this time. James stretched and rose from his bed. Outside their simple home, whispered voices could be heard as the men of the fleet made their way down to the boats.

"I'm guessing it's time to depart, Matt. I can hear voices and see fire torches down by the boats."

"We ought to take some food with us – we could be out for hours. There's still some stew, though the meat was a bit tough, but it's all we have."

"We didn't eat all of the bread either so we'll take both. Cold food is better than no food! Perhaps we should take some water too; I saw a clay water pot with a stopper in the cupboard."

They collected their things and made their way down to the boats. James was welcomed several times with cheerful greetings, but nobody greeted Matt or even made eye contact with him in the light of the flaming torches.

"I'm beginning to feel uneasy with my lack of popularity, James."

"Clearly, whatever Simon said to them last night has made little difference. It's something we need to get to the bottom of, and I've already decided to speak to Simon about it when I get the chance. Keep your chin up, Matt. Think of it like the start of a rugby match where we all make eye contact to try and psych each other out."

"Good idea. If they won't talk to me then I can at least make them feel uncomfortable about it!"

"I have never known anybody better at that particular skill," said James, laughing.

They made their way along the line of boats and found only one awaiting its occupants. Confidently, they boarded, watching as the other fishermen carefully laid out and folded their nets in the same way as the paper in a fan is folded. James followed in the same manner and Matt was quick to join in. He ignored the occasional unkind comments obviously directed at him. Instead, he held his head up and glared around, trying to see which man had said it. This defiant alertness soon persuaded the men to keep any further comments to themselves, as the water lapped at the bow of the boats in the uneasy silence.

Just then, a call went out announcing high tide and the men all leapt from their boats. A group of them crowded around the first boat, pushing it out into the water and one man jumped nimbly aboard. Moving on to the second boat, this too was quickly launched. Soon, all the boats were afloat and, as the predawn light started to glow on the horizon, sails were raised and the fleet set out for deeper water.

"That was an efficient way to launch a fleet I have to say," said James as his boat trailed at the rear of the fleet.

"It was, but I thought that each boat would go its own way, didn't you?"

"Things do seem a little different here to how we'd have expected, but we are talking about fishing traditions from a long time ago, so why wouldn't they be different? People survived, though, so they must be doing alright."

"If they fish as a group, then we might not know what to do when we have to act."

"I'm not particularly worried about that because we always seem to be able to do what we need to, when it's needed."

"Yeah, I guess so, but with all this hostility towards me, the last thing I want is to do something wrong."

"Don't worry, Matt – I have your back covered, you can count on that."

The fleet sailed on through the brightening dawn, but progress was slow as there was only a gentle breeze. By mid-afternoon, the climbing temperatures were checked when the wind suddenly freshened, causing the wooden boats to rock alarmingly. The fleet changed course and headed into the current, but their speed bled off dramatically. Then, a shout from the lead boat reached Matt and James, carried by the wind, and they saw the boats begin to lower their sails. James watched carefully, copying their actions. Only a small part of the sail was left raised and it wasn't long before he knew the reason why. The boats manoeuvred themselves into a rough circle and started to pour out their nets. They kept moving slowly around in a circle which extended the nets fully.

Shortly after, the boats started to close up, making the circle much smaller. Fish began to jump out of the water as the hidden shoal was herded up. The tighter the circle, the more the fish jumped, until the frenzy was constant. Then, on a shout from the lead boat, which was now immediately to James' and Matt's left, they started to haul in the nets. The strain on their arms was immense, until they somehow managed to find a rhythm that mirrored the rocking motion of the boat. Even so, it still required an enormous effort.

The men on the lead boat could barely haul in their nets; such was the huge bounty of fish it contained. Matt watched it to take his mind off his own physical struggles. Suddenly, one of the two men lost his grip on the net. The sudden release of pressure sent him reeling backwards, his head striking the mast with a sickening blow. He teetered slowly, before his knees buckled as he fell backwards into the water.

The cry of "Man overboard!" carried clearly, and it seemed as if time stood still as the fishermen watched in horror. A lungful of air kept the man afloat for the moment, but he was lying face down in the water and, as the men watched, a long shadow just under the surface could be seen gliding towards him.

Matt hadn't seen the shadow; he was struggling to understand why the man's partner hadn't jumped in to save him. Acting purely on instinct, he ran the two or three steps towards the bow of the boat and launched himself into the water. It was a perfect swallow dive that an Olympic champion would have been proud of. He arched his back to keep the dive as shallow as possible, immediately finding his stride. He covered the short distance in next to no time and had soon turned the unconscious man over to get his face out of the water. Three powerful strokes later and he was at the side of the leading boat where the remaining fisherman grabbed his friend under the armpits and pulled him out of danger.

Instantly, a cry of alarm went up and Matt turned to see something large closing in on him. He ducked straight under the water to confront his would-be attacker. Opening his eyes, he found himself almost paralysed with shock at what he saw. The beast that swam by him was enormous – at least four metres long. There was certainly no mistaking a crocodile when you saw one and this one was easily capable of severing an arm or leg, if not worse. As the crocodile turned and started towards him again, the sweeping tail had an almost mesmeric effect on him. He had to keep watch, but he badly needed air.

The water above him became turbulent and he risked a quick gaze upward to see the water being beaten with several oars. Reaching out, he grabbed one into the water, turning the blade towards the reptile. The momentary action had diverted his attention from the beast and he was only just in time to see it hurtling towards him, about a metre away. The creature opened its mouth revealing jagged white teeth, and closed its eyes at the last second when it expected to make contact with its prey. Matt, judging the moment perfectly, rammed the oar with all his force into the mouth of the crocodile, which clamped its jaws shut, immediately thrashing to and fro, and wrenching the other end of the oar violently from his grip. Matt swam quickly upwards, breaking the surface at speed and gulping in great lungfuls of air, as several pairs of hands reached down, grabbing whatever part of him they could, and unceremoniously plucking him from the water.

It took Matt several seconds of panting, leaning down into the bottom of the boat before the realisation of what had just happened hit him. He also became aware of the silence surrounding him, and raised his head to see the worry etched on James' face and a number of fishermen aboard their boat, staring at him.

He smiled, wiping water from his nose with the back of his hand.

"Well," he announced, "that was a close one!"

His words seemed to break the spell and the sound of relieved laughter filled the air.

"You ok, Matt?" asked James, anxiously.

"I'm fine thanks to you and everyone else, the injured man – is he all right?"

"Look over there," said James, gesturing.

Matt looked across to the neighbouring boat to see a man receiving a rough bandage to the head. Noticing Matt, he raised his hand and then simply gave a slow deliberate nod.

"If that doesn't gain you a few friends, then we're not going to stay in this community a moment longer," James told him supportively.

"Well, either way, we've got to get the nets back in before we can leave," said Matt, and gave his familiar laugh of victory that he used whenever their team had won a match.

Forgiveness

The catch was huge and caused many to raise an eyebrow in surprise. In fact, there was more than enough for the villagers, so Simon suggested taking some to the next inland village for selling before they spoiled in the heat.

Matt and James continued to follow the example of the other fishermen, doing whatever they did and laid out their nets in the sand too. This dried the nets as well as any bits of weed and other foreign objects that had become attached. Once brittle, they were much easier to remove later on. It also allowed the men to see and repair any damage to the nets; their haul had been so big that some of the fragile knots had been broken, forming holes through which even large fish would be able to escape. James hoped to learn the repairing skill that all the men here had known since childhood.

When the fishermen started to disperse and head to their homes, James and Matt followed suit. They were tired from the hard day's work, not to mention the adrenaline surge from the encounter with the crocodile.

A woman knocked at their door just before darkness and James opened it.

"Hello, James. I've come to say thank you to your friend for saving my husband's life."

"Your thanks are appreciated, but are really not necessary. Matt did what all decent people should do and that is simply helping those who need it, when they need it."

"It sounds like you've been listening to the Rabbi, James! I'm sure he used those words a few weeks ago, when I heard one of his talks."

"If the Rabbi said those words, it is proof that what I said is right."

"I would still like to thank Matthew in person, if you would invite me in."

"Of course, how rude of me! It just goes to show how tired I am from working so hard today."

"It was a truly amazing catch. You were indeed blessed."

"Matt, I have a friend here who wishes to speak to you."

"Shalom, Matthew. I am Martha, wife of Jarrod, the man whose life you saved with your brave actions today."

"How is he Martha? I do hope he's feeling better now."

"It is good of you to show such concern for the welfare of another. Jarrod is not one to complain, though I believe he still suffers a little from shock. But the knock he took to the head should heal well.

"That's good, then he will be back out on the sea very soon."

"Thanks to you, he will be."

"It wasn't only me, Martha. Other hands also offered help."

"It was only you who dared defy the creatures of the deep to save him. It is rare that a crocodile should range so far north, but it is not the first that has been spotted here. I can think of at least two occasions during my childhood when one was seen. I hope the others learn from the selflessness you displayed today."

"I might not have been so brave had I thought about my actions before I carried them out," admitted Matt, ruefully.

"In that case, Matthew, I am thankful that you have an impetuous nature. I will take my leave now, but I wanted you to have this."

She handed over a blanket that Matt had mistakenly thought was a night wrap. It had been beautifully made from squares of tightly woven wool and boasted several colours which weren't used on their own drab coloured blankets.

"This is very beautiful, Martha. You must have spent many hours creating this. It is too much – I could not possibly accept this."

"But you must! This is my most treasured possession except one."

"What is the one you value most?"

"My husband, of course! He also insists that you have this."

"In that case, I have no choice. I promise I will take good care of it, for it is truly a thing of great beauty."

Martha smiled at the compliments paid to her handiwork, bade them both goodnight and left.

"Well, that's the first positive thing that has happened to me since we got here, James."

"No more than you deserve for your bravery."

"Maybe, but you would have done the same."

"Of course, but you were always quicker at thinking on your feet and acting instantaneously."

"True, buddy, but then you have other skills that are better than mine, and that's what makes us such a good team!"

The next morning, they awoke much later. Dawn had already broken and James decided to fetch some fresh water, while Matt savoured a few more minutes on his bunk. As he approached the well, he saw the tall, elegant figure of Simon winding the handle to retrieve his bucket.

"Shalom, James! Did you rest well?"

"Shalom, Simon! I had forgotten how tiring fishing was, I have to confess."

"Indeed! I have news to share with you. I have spoken with the community once more on behalf of your friend. I told them that the manner in which he had been treated was not merited and that it was not how we should treat visitors to our village. I said, also, that if you could find it in your heart to forgive him, James, then we should do the same. And finally, I reminded them of his brave and selfless actions in preventing the loss of one of our own yesterday, and that the gift of a life far outweighs any past wrongdoings."

"What did the people say?"

"It was agreed that he should and will be treated in a manner in which all men would like to be treated, from this day forward. Is that not good news?"

"It is the best news. I will tell Matthew when I return."

"There will be no need for you to tell him anything, for when he comes out of your house, he will receive gifts from all the fishermen's families."

"We already received a gift from Martha last night, and that is more than enough thanks."

"The truth is, James, these men are not simply giving a gift of gratitude, but also asking for forgiveness for misjudging him."

"I think the community is stronger for having a man like you to guide them, Simon."

"It is good of you to say so, but I too have somebody who guides me."

"Would that be the Rabbi who Martha was telling us about last night?"

"You are most perceptive! It is my desire to take you to listen to him when he returns from his travels."

James took his turn to fill his water containers as he continued the conversation with Simon. Although his ulterior motive was to find out as much as he could that might suggest a purpose for their visit to the village, he also found he could speak to the big, gentle man with an ease that surprised him.

"We should go back. The women need to prepare food to break our fast, as well as enough for tomorrow. Since we have introduced the non-working Sabbath day, the community has found time to share and join in activities that would not have been possible before. It has forged stronger links between all the families here and the friendships have grown stronger. The community's needs have been promoted above those of the individual, and disputes are less common these days. It is good to belong to such a group of people, do you not think, James?"

"I do and I hope that it lasts."

"There is no reason why it should not!"

They walked back towards the house and James noticed a small crowd talking to Matt.

"I hope there is no trouble there."

"There will be none, of that I am sure," reassured Simon.

As they approached closer, Matt was saying Shalom to the last of the group who had come bearing gifts.

"Look at all this, James – the people here are truly generous!"

"You risked your life to save one of them and that is not to be taken lightly. I, too, have a gift for you and will bring it to you later today," Simon told him.

"Will you not stay to have breakfast with us, Simon? I have been given bread, cheese and dried fish among this pile of gifts. What is the good of having things if you cannot share them?"

"That is a sentiment which I hold dear and so I will gladly help you lighten your supply," said Simon, grinning. "If that cheese was made by the person I think it was, then you will find none finer, hereabouts!"

They helped Matt take in the gifts he had received and then the three of them sat outside, eating their breakfast. People passed their house frequently, which surprised both Matt and James because the only thing beyond was the sea and, as far as they could tell, nobody was going there. Everyone that passed said 'Shalom' to Matt and gave him a smile.

"It seems you have become a favourite overnight!" said Simon, as three children passed by for the third time in ten minutes.

They were still talking an hour after they had finished eating, and had been joined by one or two other fisherman with whom they had been out on the sea yesterday. The conversation was about nothing in particular and was effortlessly companionable.

"This reminds me of in-season training nights after the training is finished, when we all hang out together, just because we can," commented Matt quietly to James, who nodded thoughtfully.

There came a shout from somewhere in the distance, followed by a couple of screams that broke the peaceful nature of the gathering.

Some of the men stood up, which prompted the rest of them to follow suit, including Matt and James.

"It came from over there!" exclaimed one of the men, who ran off in the direction of the commotion.

Two more screams shrilled out and the men broke into a trot. A child came running past with a petrified look on his face; two others pursued the first, also with faces masked with fear; then the sound of a whip cracking, and another scream. They rounded a building, coming face to face with an immense bear of a man. In his left hand, he was clasping a small boy by a handful of hair, and in the other, held by the coils of his whip wrapping around her wrist, was a small girl.

"Thieving little brats!" he shouted in a booming voice.

The two ensnared children continued to wail and scream as they fought against their captor. James immediately saw red and charged at the much larger man. His attack did not have the desired effect, however, and he was caught and held effortlessly. But in doing so he had at least forced the man to let go of the children.

"What do you think you're doing?" The giant asked angrily, before raising James up above his head and launching him through the air to land several feet away in a dishevelled heap.

"I could ask you the same thing," James growled, trying hard to regain the breath that had been knocked out of him on impact with the ground. "What could these small children, not a quarter of your size, possibly have done to you to deserve such treatment?"

The two suddenly freed children fled between the legs of the crowd that had gathered around them.

"They stole from me – not that it is any of your business. They stole my bread and my cheese!"

"And why would they do that?"

"I am not interested in why, just the fact that they did," he said, his anger increasing again. "Now, thanks to you, I can't even punish them. Maybe I should punish you instead!"

"Don't even think about it!" said Matt, pushing his way through the crowd to stand at his friend's side.

"That goes for me too, Jeremiah!" said a man, taking a stance alongside the two young men.

"And me," said another.

Jeremiah considered taking his frustration out on James instead, but on weighing up his chances against all those now opposing him, he decided against it.

"I would be happy to share my bread and cheese with you," Matt offered in an effort to calm the man's temper.

Jeremiah stared at him, before asking. "Do you mock me?"

"My offer was sincere, Jeremiah."

"Keep your bread and stay away from me. And you – especially you." he said trying to out-stare James.

James met the look full-on, his temper not yet abated.

Then suddenly Jeremiah turned and left. "Not a very nice person, is he?" James commented, to nobody in particular.

The Plight of the Homeless Children

"Do not prejudge Jeremiah, James, for there is much about that man that you do not understand. Although I do not condone his actions, there are reasons why he is as he appears," said Simon, a short while later.

"Whatever his reasons, they cannot possibly justify him beating small children," declared Matt, hotly.

"Tell us about him, Simon. If he has problems, then maybe we could do something to help him," said James, kicking himself for doing the very thing that everybody had been doing to Matt.

"It is neither the time nor the place, James, and if I do tell you without good reason, then I would be betraying a confidence that was entrusted to me."

"I would not want you to do that but, if there is a way to help Jeremiah, then I would genuinely like to. A man that would hurt children over a little food must have a real problem inside. I don't need his story to find a reason to help him."

"You are considerate, James, of both him and me. We will talk of this another time – of that I promise."

"Why did those children try to steal his food?" interrupted Matt, suddenly curious to know the reason for this petty theft.

"They steal for many reasons, Matthew, but mostly because they are hungry."

"Don't their parents give them enough to eat? I mean, I know things are hard, but surely people are not so poor as to be unable to feed their children?"

"Again, all is not as it seems. The children you saw have no families or anybody else to care for them. Many have been abandoned; some have lost their parents to illness and death; and others have wandered in from neighbouring villages where they have similar numbers of these poor wretches."

"How many are we talking about, exactly?" Matt pursued.

"There are probably about ten or so that frequent our village and the next one, and more of them choose to live in the hills, too."

"Do they have anywhere to sleep or keep warm on a winter's night?"

"Unfortunately, they do not. Most survive by finding shelter inland away from the coastal breezes during the winter months, but they are forced to come into the villages in search of whatever people leave out for them, or what they can scavenge or, if the need is greater, then what they are able to steal. The people here are not without sympathy and give what they can, but nobody can afford to take on another child, especially if they have some of their own. Pilot's demand for taxes is insatiable and if his demands are not met, the young may be taken for slaves by the Roman soldiers."

"If I were to meet this pilot, I would like to give him a piece of my mind," declared Matt, angrily.

"I would like to know how a pilot has so much power that he can demand so much from the people," James added.

"There are many who think as you do, Matthew, but to do so would invite certain death. In the world we live in, we have to fight, but our fight is about surviving, and that takes all we have to give."

"Do you think that the people who gave me gifts of food earlier would be upset if I shared it out among the children?"

"Not one of them would complain; no doubt it would be

viewed in the same light as your good deed yesterday."

"In that case, Simon, if you will excuse me, I will tend to it right away. Are you coming with me, James?"

James nodded and the two of them bade shalom to Simon and left him watching them as they hurried away.

"What the heck were you thinking, taking on that giant all by yourself? That's the kind of thing you're always having a go at *me* for doing! It wasn't like you at all. *Normal* James would have thought about it and realised that he was just too big to attack by himself. We *both* took on Little John and that's how we won, remember?"

"You're right Matt, I'm sorry. It's just that, well, he was attacking little kids, and I just got angry. I am allowed to do that occasionally, aren't I?" His voice was full of passion, clearly the anger hadn't dissipated fully yet.

"Of course you are and I'm sorry to have a go. I was just worried, that's all. Actually, it's nice to see that you can also make the wrong decision every now and then, instead of leaving that to me all the time."

James gave a short laugh and then looked at his friend thoughtfully.

"You acted out of character too, you know, up in the hills, hiding from the soldiers instead of going to meet them."

"So I did," Matt grinned, "does this mean all this time travelling is changing us?"

"No! More likely that we're just rubbing off on each other more these days." James laughed, and Matt joined in.

"Let's go and find some children to feed."

There was more than enough bread to go round, but the cheese would be stretched thin. James placed it in an empty bucket, for want of anything else to carry it in, and the two of them headed off in the direction the children had taken when fleeing from Jeremiah.

As the village fell further from view, the pair started to climb upwards towards the pastureland and, in particular, a rocky outcrop bordered by a clump of thick bushes on two sides.

"Do you see them, Matt?"

"I saw them some time ago, but I'm guessing they saw us the minute we left the village. The closer we get to them, the more they seem to be hiding. It's a bit like when you go paintballing – you just get a glimpse of them every now and then.

"You can't really blame them, after what Jeremiah tried to do to them."

"Something tells me that they risk that every time they're forced to steal, and not just from Jeremiah."

They approached the bushes, knowing full well that the children were present, although expertly hidden within a few metres of them.

"We know you're there! We have food with us, and if you'd like to share it, I suggest you come out and sit with us. You have my word that we won't harm you," called James.

They waited patiently, before Matt tried a different tactic. Taking a piece of cheese and a hunk of bread from the bucket, he held it up and took a large bite of the bread.

"Mmmm, this bread is really good! James, you should try some with a piece of cheese."

Suddenly, he felt a strong yank on the bucket that almost wrenched it from his hand.

"What the heck?" he said, lifting up the bucket, as well as the small, thin child clinging to it.

"What do we have here then? I don't know – we invite them to lunch and still they try to steal it! If you wish to eat, come out and sit with us."

The boy holding on to the bucket released his clutch on it. He couldn't have been more than ten or eleven but was incredibly thin, his ribcage clearly visible beneath his skin. Matt gently lowered the boy who didn't run away; instead, he cautiously sat a short distance from Matt.

"What's your name, boy?" asked Matt, curiously.

"I have not been called by my name for a long time, but it used to be David."

"Shalom, David. I am Matthew and my friend here is

James."

Matt offered him some bread and a small piece of cheese.

"I'm sorry, we don't have much cheese and, if I give you any more, there won't be enough for your friends. If, of course, they're as brave as you and are prepared to come and sit with us," said Matt, laying down the challenge in a theatrically loud voice.

He and James made a few more satisfied noises when, from positions remarkably close to them, half a dozen children revealed themselves. They sat down with James and Matt and each received a portion of bread and cheese which they wolfed down voraciously.

When the food had all gone, the children left silently, without saying a word of thanks. All except for David.

"There isn't any more food, David," said James, showing the boy the empty bucket.

The boy said nothing but remained seated alongside Matt. With the other children gone, there was little point in staying there, so Matt and James rose to return to the village.

"We're going home now, David. Don't you want to go back to your friends?" asked Matt.

"You're the one the whole village is talking about – the one who fights with crocodiles," said David suddenly with a smile.

Matt nodded. "Although, it wasn't really like that…"

"Now you give all your food to homeless children. You are not like other men. I've watched you. You do good things and everybody is good to you in return. Perhaps if I do something good, people would be kind to me in the same way."

"What do you have in mind, David?"

"I do not know yet, but if I listen carefully, then someone may need something and perhaps then I will be able to help."

"People do not have much to give here, David, but you already know that, don't you?"

"I do not need much to live on. There was a time when I wanted to herd goats, like the boy you passed the other day, but the soldiers have taken his herd for themselves and will make a slave of him.

"And I do not wish to be a slave for anyone," he added dejectedly.

Matt and James both drew sharp intakes of breath as they swallowed the news of the little goat herder's plight.

"If we'd only known what was happening, we might have been able to help," said James, angrily.

Matt nodded his agreement, the rage he felt was written all over his face.

A short while later, they bade David shalom and set off back to the village, but after a few minutes, they realised he was following them. Saying nothing, they continued on their way. Even as they walked along the beach, they knew that the boy was still behind them and still they did not turn around. They passed a few people who each greeted them personally, and Matt smiled with pleasure that he was no longer being viewed with hostility.

As they approached their dwelling, they saw a bucket, full of fish in water standing at one side.

"Tonight's dinner, by the look of it," said James, taking it inside. Matt followed and shut the door behind him.

"Is the boy still there?" asked James.

Matt poked his head out of one of the small windows and looked down to see the boy sitting close to the door, not looking like he was going anywhere very soon. He nodded to James.

"Maybe for the duration of the time we're here, we can at least take care of him and give him a little to eat every now and then."

"Yeah, we'll do what we can – no child should live like this," agreed Matt, still agitated at the plight of the youngsters.

"It's a different time and a different culture, Matt, we can't be too judgemental."

"I know, I know. But it grates on me."

"Let's prepare some of this fish for tonight. Perhaps we can show these people how we do it where we're from."

"What do you have in mind?"

"If we can rustle up some olive oil and flour, we could give the fish a coating of flour before frying them. It's my Dad's favourite; he even eats them cold the next day, if there's any left over."

"I'm up for that, but since you're flavour of the month around these parts, I'll let you scrounge whatever we need, while I clean the fish."

"No need for that, my friend! They're already prepared – I noticed it earlier. They aren't filleted yet, but the guts have been removed."

"Well, that means my job's done then, and we're just waiting for you!"

"Enjoy your moment while you can, James, because the next task will be your responsibility."

James laughed and watched Matt head off, noticing David follow him from a discreet distance.

A few minutes later, he returned with the supplies he needed.

"Let's make a fire out here; we can fry them without smelling out the house," he suggested.

"David! Do you think you can collect some wood for us, please?" James asked the small boy, as he made his appearance.

He nodded and disappeared, returning with his arms full of branches and large twigs.

Matt started to coat the fish in flour as soon as they were filleted. His fingers quickly became clogged in the sticky floury mixture, so David helped him, until he too found his fingers so gummed up, it was difficult to grip the fish pieces. They were both laughing as they went to wash the sticky goo from their fingers. James poured a little of the precious oil into the bottom of the cooking pot and, by the time they had cleaned themselves up, James had started frying the fish.

The smells from the pan drew many of the women interested in sampling the fish and seeing how it had been prepared. James enjoyed the attention and was patient with his explanations. When the cooking was over, and with enough left over for the following day, the boys decided to turn in for the night. They extinguished the fire and covered the embers in sand, then turned to enter the house. By the side of the door, David had fallen asleep.

"I am going to make him a bed inside, Matt. Give me a minute and bring him in."

"That's a great idea."

The Soldiers' Visit

Early the next morning, when Matt and James woke, they found that David had already left. There was a pile of wood stacked neatly outside the doorway and two full buckets of fresh water. The left-over cooked fish had gone though. James commented on it to Matt.

"Looks like the boy is trying to earn his food; fresh water and wood!"

"He's taken all the food, though, and that was worth more than his labour."

"My guess is that he took it for the other children."

"It's no way to live, is it James?" replied Matt, ruefully.

"No, it isn't. Listen, I overheard some of the fishermen talking about cleaning and repairing the nets today, ready for another fishing trip tomorrow. So I think we should tag along, you know, play the part of dedicated fishermen."

"OK, but I want to try and find out some more about that character Jeremiah. Simon as good as spoke up for him yesterday, despite the abuse he was dishing out to the kids."

"Maybe we can get some information from Jarrod. He owes you, Matt, and might well talk to you. Perhaps you could drop the subject casually into a conversation about the state of his injuries. Why is it that you're so hung up about Jeremiah?"

"Just a gut instinct, but I get the feeling that he's really suffering, and I'd like to help him."

"I was thinking that Simon might be the one who needs our assistance, especially as he seems to be the leader of the community."

"Realistically, it could be either of them. No one else we've met has spent more than a few minutes with us."

"But then, neither has Jeremiah."

"I know, but I just have that feeling."

The morning passed with both of them cleaning and repairing their nets. Although the task was mundane, both James and Matt once again enjoyed discovering that they had innate skills they had not had previously. One of the strange perks of their time-travelling adventures was that they retained any skills they learned even after they returned home to their own time.

They finished their work before some of the others, so split up to help fishermen who were still working. James went to the nearest boat, while Matt went to seek out Jarrod.

"Shalom, Jarrod!" called Matt as he approached the lead boat.

Jarrod rose to greet Matt and the two stood head to head.

"It's good to see that your injuries have not prevented your ability to work," said Matt, smiling.

Jarrod reached out his hands and clasped Matt's forearm.

"Shalom, Matthew. My wounds are insignificant, just a slight headache. But I am still living my life, thanks to your bravery. I am indeed in your debt."

Matt told him that he and James had finished their net so it was a good opportunity to come and talk. He bent down and began to pull out the now brittle weed and small crustaceans that clung to the net. Jarrod bent down beside him and the conversation started to flow in the easy manner of men at work. They discussed many things before heading back into the village after they had finished their task. Matt had noticed James go over to Simon's boat and saw them both leaving for the village some time ago. He knew that his friend would be finding out as much as he could.

On reaching the houses, he left Jarrod to continue towards his own dwelling and went inside to see if James was there. He was disappointed to see that he wasn't, especially as he was eager to share the information he'd uncovered about Jeremiah.

A small figure appeared at the doorway.

"There is something that I could help you with, Matthew?"

"For the moment there is nothing, thank you David. But I will call for you the minute I need your help."

David smiled with pleasure, knowing that an understanding had been reached between the two of them.

"If you seek James, he is at the home of Simon," he said casually.

Matt nodded and indicated for David to sit beside him.

"How many children are in your group?" he asked.

"I do not know for sure, as some come and go at different times, but there are at least two of us for every boat there is on the beach."

"It must be hard for you to find food in the winter months."

"It is hard for everybody to find food in the winter months, especially when the seas are too rough for the boats to go out."

"Wouldn't you like to have a place that you can call home?"

"I may not have a roof over my head, but this place is my home. We all feel this and it is why we do not leave. When we are older, we will build boats of our own and join the others on the beach. Until then, we will live as we do now."

Just as he finished his last words, a scream from somewhere in the village reached their ears, followed by shouting.

"Something's happening," offered Matt, unnecessarily.

"The soldiers have returned."

"What do they want?"

"What they always want – food and money. And they will take the small ones to be sold for slaves, if they do not get enough."

"I must go and find James, and you must hide, David. Go

down to the boats and wait until these men go. I will let you know when they've gone."

David didn't hesitate and ran off quickly.

Matt watched him safely disappear between a couple of boats, before turning and walking towards the increasing sound of angry voices. He rounded a small house and saw the crowd that had gathered.

There were five soldiers, brandishing their swords threateningly, facing a group of villagers at least six times as many. The soldiers appeared unsteady on their feet, swaying slightly from side to side. Simon was standing in front of them, trying to convince them to put away their swords.

One of the soldiers took a pace forward and swung a fist into Simon's face. The fisherman maintained his balance and took the blow without trying to protect himself.

An angry roar emitted from the crowd and Jeremiah made his way to the front. He strode towards the soldier who had struck Simon and, with immense strength, lifted him effortlessly above his head and threw him towards the other four soldiers. The soldier sailed through the air with flailing arms and legs, before crashing into two of the others. Quickly, they got to their feet and immediately encircled Jeremiah, who snarled angrily at them, like a wounded bear.

They charged Jeremiah as a single unit from all directions, and the big man fell to the ground with such force that those close enough felt it shake. The soldiers fell on top of him, smashing the hilts of their swords into his head and body and beating him even after he had lost consciousness.

Matt launched himself into action and dragged away one of the soldiers from Jeremiah's prone body. He ordered three fishermen to stand over him and prevent him from re-joining the attack. He repeated his actions again with a second soldier, before two fishermen dragged off a third. James suddenly appeared on the scene and took care of the fourth, and then a loud voice called a command so loud that nobody, apart from the soldiers, understood what it meant.

Many faces turned to see a Roman officer on a beautiful

white stallion. A red cloak covered his back but fell to the sides at the front revealing silver-coloured armour plating that covered his whole torso. A pleated tunic hung to just below his knees and his feet were dressed in leather footwear unlike anything Matt and James had ever seen before. The man was very handsome with a fine physique, judging by the muscles of his legs.

"Release those soldiers, immediately!" he ordered the villagers.

"If we let them go, Tribune, there is no telling what they'll do next as they are under the influence of too much wine," said Simon, walking toward the mounted figure.

"If that is so, they will be punished. How did all this start?"

"They came demanding food and money, of which we have neither. They refused to believe us and attempted to dishonour some of the women. When we tried to stop them, they responded with violence and threatened to take our children to be sold as slaves."

"And this man who has been beaten?" he asked, pointing at the unconscious Jeremiah.

"This man tried to prevent this happening."

"He is brave to have taken on five soldiers, but it is foolish and against the law to attack a member of the Roman army. By the look of him, he is almost dead, so I decree that he has already received his punishment. The conduct of my men has also been unacceptable, and for that, they too will be punished. Caesar would expect no less of his soldiers than to behave in the manner of civilised Roman citizens, in peacetime."

Again, Tribune shouted a strident order to the soldiers. Immediately, they assumed a formation and stood to attention, before barking a further command which set them moving in double time to keep pace with the his horse.

As soon as they had disappeared behind some houses, four men moved forward and carried the unfortunate Jeremiah by his limbs to the largest building in the village.

Built as a communal building, this was at least four times

bigger than the structure that James and Matt were calling home. Inside it was a large main space with a smaller room at one end which, since it was completely empty, did not betray the purpose of its existence.

Blankets appeared from nowhere and a rough bed was made up, before Jeremiah's body was laid down upon it. Two women carrying water and cloths emerged at the front of the small crowd that had followed into the room and immediately set about tending Jeremiah's wounds. As they worked, everybody sat down, patiently waiting for a sign that he would be alright.

Simon stood up and faced those who sat waiting. He invited them to pray and everybody clasped their hands together and closed their eyes. Looking nervously around, but feeling the need to be part of this, Matt and James followed Simon's invitation, surprised at the strength of their own concerns and worries, but aware of how this connected every member of the community present. The prayers went on for some minutes before a little cry from one of the two nurses encouraged Simon to issue an 'Amen'.

The woman said something to him in a quiet voice as he stooped over to look at the heavily bruised face of Jeremiah. Then he straightened and made the announcement that everyone wanted to hear.

"It is clear that God has answered our prayers. Jeremiah still lives and, although his wounds are many and will give him pain for some time, there are no broken bones. Our God is a merciful God."

With the announcement over, the seated community rose and slowly left the building leaving only Simon, the two nurses and Matt and James present.

"You took a risk attacking the soldiers," Simon declared, in a voice that was neither approving nor disapproving.

Matt looked at him and nodded his head.

"I couldn't help myself. It seems to be my way. I always act first and think later."

"Your actions may just have saved Jeremiah's life, but the

soldiers won't forget this. I fear their lust for power is all-consuming."

7

Tribune Artemus Septavia

Angrily, Tribune Artemus Septavia led his five soldiers away at a steady canter. He kept the pace up for some miles to punish the men who had embarrassed the Roman army and, more importantly, his legion. The men laboured heavily now and he felt tempted to use his whip on them, but he was not without mercy.

Halting his journey, he dismounted, untying his water carrier even before his feet touched the ground. Throwing it to the first soldier in the ragged line that followed him, he motioned for them to sit down and proceeded to lecture them on the standard of behaviour he expected from all his men. To discourage any further incidents, he ended with a personal threat of his own should any of the five reoffend. They listened dutifully, if woodenly, and did not go unnoticed by the Tribune. He wondered if any of his speech had been absorbed and whether the men would obey.

He sighed, discouraged, remounted his horse and continued along the trail. The garrison was camped just a mile away and he was looking forward to leaving his men for the few days' leave he was about to start, for he sorely needed it.

Arriving at their destination, he soon spotted Decanus Lucius Asina and immediately looked away in distaste. The man stared at him defiantly and disrespectfully, despite his lower rank. The Decanus represented everything Artemus despised in both a man and a soldier, for he was vicious and cruel, without remorse or compassion; a man hell-bent on furthering his career at whatever cost. His most notable achievements were the destruction of Rome's so-called enemies, people who, in truth, were nothing more than downtrodden civilians incapable of fighting back. This included the rounding up of children as potential slaves; a task he took to with relish and one at which no other could beat him. Artemus knew that one day the man would challenge him for his position, and that he would have to fight him to the death.

Endless travel and fighting throughout the past five years had taken its toll on Artemus' mind, and he longed for the opportunity to go back home to Rome to see the wife who would be like a stranger to him now, and the child he had never met.

Today seemed to be something of a turning point for him, however, for the decision that had long thwarted him had finally been made. There was little he needed to do and little he needed to take. A wrap holding the few belongings that he wished to take with him was secured by leather straps, which he slipped onto his shoulder so that the bag clung to his side and rested onto his hip. He laid his arm upon it and headed out of the garrison.

At the same spot where he had earlier rested his men, Artemus stopped under one of the trees in the small copse, and removed his pack. Quickly, he stripped off his tunic and the rest of his Roman regalia and donned the simple robe of the common people. He fixed the hood so that it hung lower than normal and concealed his face at the slightest incline of his head, and then wrapped his clothes into his pack. Looking around to ensure he was alone, he climbed nimbly into one of the trees and placed his pack in a fork in the branches, using the straps to secure it into position. The straps were a similar colour to the bark, almost invisible against the branch unless you knew what you were looking for. Satisfied that no one could see it from below, he dropped to the ground and continued back towards the village.

He knew that he might easily be recognised and wished to reveal himself to nobody except the man called Simon. He had to see him and talk to him; only this man could help him understand the torment he felt in his heart, mind and, indeed, his very soul. Stopping on a hill just outside the village, he waited – oblivious to the insects constantly buzzing around his head that occasionally landed on his beard, causing him to scratch unwittingly.

A sixth sense suddenly told him he was no longer alone. As he focussed on listening for the slightest sound that might betray this unwanted company, a rustling in the grass to his left, too strong to be caused by the wind, finally caught his straining ears. A slight movement in the tall tussocks of grass also gave his eyes something to focus on. The next moment he pounced, cat-like, onto his prey and stood up, holding a small boy by his tattered clothing.

"Why are you sneaking up behind me, boy?" he asked, examining the filthy creature whose smell offended his nose.

"I was not sneaking up on you, I was trying to get away from you."

"Why would you fear me?"

"I do not fear you; I just do not know you. The place where you sit is where I live for most of the year."

"You live in the open, among the grass?"

"Except during the colder months of the year when I leave for the Caves of Menin."

"Isn't there a leper community there?"

"There is, but they use different caves from the one I stay in and I do not get too close to them."

"You are wise for leprosy is not a pleasant way to die. What happened to your parents?"

"I am told that they died of disease when I was very small. I don't really remember them. Once you are without family, you are left with little."

"How old are you boy?"

"I have counted seven cycles of the seasons so far, and

there were more before I learned to count."

"Who taught you to count?"

"A man who once travelled between villages and collected taxes taught me. He would give me a food for doing small tasks for him. But this man no longer collects taxes and has nothing to share with a homeless boy."

"You have had a hard life, my friend, and have done well to survive it so far. If I give you a small coin, do you think you could get food enough for both of us?"

"What makes you think that I would return with the food and not keep it for myself?"

"If you did that, then you would lose the opportunity of it happening again."

The boy considered the man's words before agreeing with the sense they made.

"If I am to do this for you, what shall I call you?"

"You can call me Arte. It is a shorter version of my full name."

"You can call me Michael. I took the name of a fisherman friend, who lost his life at sea, as I didn't know my real name. Each time he went to sea he gave me some of his catch, even when the catch was poor."

"It sounds like you had a good friend there."

"That is the truth, but like anything good that ever happens to me, it quickly comes to an end and I end up right back where I started."

The Tribune nodded in understanding, before sending Michael on his way. After he had gone, he returned to his vigil of waiting and watching, his eyes constantly searching for the one called Simon.

He was still in the same place, when Michael returned with some bread and cheese.

"It seems I was right to trust you and, as you have not let me down, I invite you to sit by my side and share the food you have bought for me."

The pair ate in silence as the light began to dim. It was a strange silence, for neither felt uncomfortable with it, even though they knew so little about each other. When they had eaten all the food, the Tribune posed the question he had been waiting to ask.

"Do you know the man they call Simon, a fisherman who sails from this village?"

Michael nodded.

"What is he like?"

"He is a good and kind man. He often leaves food from his catch for the children from the hills."

"Do you mean all the children who have no homes or family?"

Michael nodded. "The fishermen of this village have always been good to me and my friends, except for one, who often whips us with little cause."

"What do you do to anger this man?"

"Steal. When there is not enough food to go round, we are forced to steal to stay alive. We do not want to, but we have no choice. Every winter one of us dies of hunger or an illness they are too weak to fight off."

"Tell me more about Simon."

"Simon has helped us when no other has. He will give away his last piece of bread if he thinks we need it more. He has saved us many times from the whip of Jeremiah. There is little more to say; he has no wife or child of his own but fishes with his brother, Andrew, who I believe is his only family."

"You have been a great help to me, Michael, but I seek one more favour from you – a favour that I am willing to pay for."

"What is it that I can do for you?"

"I want to meet with Simon, here, away from other people. It is my wish to speak with him as, I believe, he has answers to questions that I cannot answer myself."

"Are you going to hurt Simon?"

"Good grief, no! It is as I say; he is the man to answer my questions. I have seen him with others and know that his heart is pure and good, so can tell me the truth."

"What will you give me for arranging this?"

"I will give you another coin, like the one I gave you for

food, when you return with him. But he must come alone, for my conversation with him must remain private."

Michael nodded and, once again, headed off to the village.

While he was gone, the Tribune collected wood and built a small fire which he lit as soon as the sun finally dropped below the horizon. He sat close to it, in a bid to offset the chill of twilight.

Michael returned an hour later.

"Arte, it is me, Michael! I have Simon with me."

"Step into the light and warmth of the fire, Michael, and bring Simon with you."

"There is one other with us, a friend of Simon's, called James."

Arte tensed at the news. This was expressly not what he had asked for.

"Why have you brought another, Simon?" he asked, cautiously. "I asked that you come alone. The words that I wish to speak to you are from my heart and are not for others to hear."

"You have nothing to fear from James, Arte, for his heart is good. I believe we may both be of help to you."

Arte hesitated, before gesturing the two men forward.

Sitting down close to the fire, the two newcomers held their hands to the flames, revelling in its comforting warmth. The man they had agreed to meet was sitting with a hood concealing his face.

"Shalom Simon, Shalom James. Let me introduce myself – I am Arte."

"I recognise your voice. You have no need to conceal your face from us, Tribune," said James in surprise.

The Tribune removed his hood and stared uncompromisingly into James' eyes. It was as if he wanted to see inside his very soul, but he met the gaze of a good and honest man and was reassured.

"You are not dressed in the clothes of a Roman Tribune, Arte," commented Simon.

"You are correct, Simon, but I have not come here with

the intention of spying. My mission is simple; to talk with someone I believe can make sense of what I am feeling, who could perhaps offer some advice about an uncertain future."

"It would appear that there is weight and confusion in your heart that troubles you."

"It goes beyond that; I find that my role in life and everything I have achieved are being challenged."

"And the way in which you have achieved those things?"

"Yes, that also, and it troubles me for I no longer fully understand what is happening to me. I no longer have direction, order or purpose for my future."

"It seems to me that we should start at the beginning. When did you first sense these feelings?"

The two men talked well into the night, with James speaking only occasionally. He sat and listened thoughtfully, still seeking an insight into Matt's and his purpose in this time and place.

It was very late when they finally returned to the village, Simon accompanied by his new friend.

Jeremiah

Jeremiah was nursed continuously by the women of the village over the next two days. Despite Simon's initially positive announcement, fears that he might never regain consciousness were increasing.

It was not until the afternoon of the third day that he finally tried to open his eyes. His wounds were substantial, especially to his upper torso, face and head, and his eyes were little more than slits, due to the extensive multi-coloured swelling around them. Considering the beating he received, many thought it was a miracle that he had not sustained serious injuries inside his body, or broken any bones. On top of this, the women feared he might also have problems with his mind once he fully regained consciousness.

At first, the poor man could not see clearly through his raw, swollen eyelids. The light in the communal space, though relatively dim, made his eyes water, and focus was impossible. Jarrod's wife, Martha, was tending him and noticed his discomfort, bathing them gently with a soft cloth, dipped in cool, clear water. She smiled at him before telling him how brave everybody thought he was in standing up to the soldiers.

He said nothing in return, lying there impassively, making no attempt to move any part of his bruised and battered body until, after a few minutes, his eyes closed in a deep, restorative sleep.

Matt had dropped by the communal space several times during that period, to check on Jeremiah's progress, and was relieved to hear that he had woken briefly. He had wanted to find out more about him, but discovered that Simon, whom he had planned to ask, had left the village for a few days with a stranger who hadn't been introduced to anybody, except James. The arrival of this mysterious man had now overtaken Jeremiah as the main topic of conversation among the villagers. It was a mystery that didn't concern Matt, however, since he knew of the hillside encounter between the three men. All the same, Simon's absence was unusually irritating for him.

It was a further two days before Jeremiah uttered his first words and made any attempt to sit up. The black and purple bruises covering his upper body had started to turn yellow, and were showing signs of fading at the edges. He had also lost weight, having been unable to eat more than a few mouthfuls of thin broth that the women had trickled gently into his mouth, so his face appeared gaunt.

He was able to thank Martha for helping raise him to a more comfortable sitting position, and sip some water carefully through his swollen lips. When he asked what had happened, she told him exactly what he'd done and how he had been severely beaten, until Matthew intervened, and the Tribune came along.

Making only a few grunts of anger under his breath at intervals throughout her retelling, Jeremiah waited until she had finished before asking to speak with Matthew.

Down at the shoreline, Matt left his task with the nets to James and made his way to the communal building. Entering, he smiled at Martha who had greeted him warmly. He accepted the goblet of cool water she offered him, promising to fetch her when he had finished talking with Jeremiah.

Martha slipped quietly out of the building, leaving the two men alone.

Jeremiah indicated for Matt to sit beside him.

"When you're feeling better, I think it would be good to

find you a more significant role here in the village. There are those of us who would like to help you with this."

"It is a thoughtful offer, but it is not just purpose and direction I lack – it's motivation."

"Why's that, Jeremiah?"

"Many things have happened in my life that makes me believe I bring trouble to those I care about. I fear that if I stay here any longer, other bad things will happen to this community."

"You do not cause these things to happen, Jeremiah; you just happen to be around when they do. What you did the other day, you did to protect people and if you hadn't taken on those soldiers, there's no telling what they might have done. Don't you see, you prevented further harm being inflicted on others? Everyone here knows it and they are very grateful to you. The women have been taking turns to nurse you; the men have also paid regular visits to see how you are faring."

"Your comments are very kind, Matthew, and I would like to believe them, as you do. I think that you are, perhaps, like me but further down the path."

"What do you mean by that?"

"Both of us have pasts we're not proud of; both of us seek to change – but you have already succeeded."

Matt thought about this before answering. He still did not know very much about his past only that his actions had caused the people here to dislike and distrust him.

"I guess everybody changes at some point or other in their lives, Jeremiah, especially when something important takes place. Sometimes the change is for the better and sometimes it is not. The way we act often reflects the way we feel inside."

"This is true. I have felt bad inside for many years and have done some unpleasant things."

"The people here do not think you are so bad."

"While I was unconscious, I had visions that I wish to discuss with Simon, but Martha tells me he is not here."

"I'm sure he won't be away for long. Were they visions or

dreams, Jeremiah?"

"Of this I cannot be sure, but they were powerful and have left me questioning the path I have taken. I believe it is time I altered direction at this seeming crossroads in my life. How were you able to achieve this, Matthew?"

Once again, Matt thought carefully before speaking. Although, he knew little about his past, he did know that he'd collected taxes for the pilot, who sounded like something of a big shot in the district. He'd never known a fisherman to be called a pilot before, but they had gone so far back in time, perhaps things were different in these times.

"There is no one thing I have done to make a big change, Jeremiah. It's more like a series of small changes that quite often go unnoticed, but still make you feel good inside. I guess it's about doing the right thing at the right time to help people. You can make a difference to individuals far easier than to a large group of people."

"Now it is *you* who is being modest, Matthew. Since you have been here, you have saved Jarrod's life, helped me with the soldiers and even stopped me hurting the children. You have won friends very quickly here."

"I have been lucky with the circumstances that came my way, plus I have James to help me stay in line when I get carried away. You need people like him around, to look out for you. There is Simon, of course – you would have talked to him about all this, had he been here."

"Perhaps you don't know; I had a child of my own once, a son, and a wife as beautiful as any woman I have ever seen."

"What happened to them?"

"They were killed, along with many others, in another village – by Roman soldiers. The soldiers were returning to their garrison after a particularly violent battle. The battle fever still raged within them as they passed through the village. They went on the rampage, leaving few behind who survived to tell the tale."

"I am so sorry for your loss, Jeremiah. That is a terrible thing to have to live with."

"She was there visiting her family, and it is worse knowing that I could not go with her as I needed to work to get money for the latest tax increase. It will be ten years this coming summer, and the pain of losing her is still as great as the day I found out."

"I cannot begin to imagine how a loss like that would feel."

"I hope you never have to experience it, Matthew, because it confuses your mind and prevents you from seeing clearly. There have been many more things that I have done during this period which I am not proud of."

"It's just grief, Jeremiah. People handle it in many different ways. In your case, you've used anger to get through a terrible period in your life."

"I will not use grief as an excuse for the things I have done."

"It's not an excuse; it's a *reason*."

"Matthew, I want you to help me change, to find a purpose in life, a reason to go on living. There has to be something I can do to help me find peace of mind, and you, more than anyone I know, might be able to help me find it. Will you help me?"

"Of course I will – and so would many others, I bet, if only you would let them. As far as finding peace of mind goes, I suggest you talk to Simon when he returns. He seems to be way ahead of anyone on that front."

"Thank you my friend. Whatever you ask me to do, I will do so, and willingly."

"But Jeremiah, I cannot make all the decisions for you. You know that, don't you? Part of changing and growing is choosing what to do for yourself, making the right choices. Right now, you just need to focus on resting and regaining your strength, so that you can face any challenge head on."

"You have a wise head for one so young."

"Wise is easy when you are not burdened in mind and heart."

Matt laid his hand on the injured man's forearm, telling him he would return later in the day. He then went to find Martha, to say that Jeremiah was feeling a little better and was probably hungry, whereon she hurried away.

When she returned, Martha sat beside Jeremiah, telling him that she had brought some of the tastiest fish stew she'd made in a long time. He looked at her and broke into a smile, the gleaming white of his teeth a perfect contrast to his jet black beard. Martha was surprised for she had never seen Jeremiah smile. Nonetheless she returned it warmly and asked him what he'd been talking to Matt about. Jeremiah shared a little of their earlier conversation, pleased to share and see the pleasure it gave Martha to be privy to a little of their conversation. He recognised this as a significant moment for him – to allow others in.

Matt wandered back down to the shore to find James as he guessed they had not yet finished repairing the nets. He greeted Jarrod as he passed by, busy at the same task, and paused to update him on Jeremiah's recovery. He suggested that the man would benefit from some kindness and friendship, so Jarrod, pleased to do something for Matt, told him that he would call in later to see him.

As Matt reached the boat to find James hard at work, a small, familiar figure appeared by his side.

"Shalom, Matthew."

"Shalom, David."

"You have been to see the big man?"

"If you mean Jeremiah, yes I have."

"He is well?"

"He is on the mend."

"I would like to visit him, with you for my protection."

"Why do you wish to visit him? And why do you think you need protection from him?"

"I stole from him in the past, before you began to give me work."

"I don't think you need to fear him anymore. In fact, I think you could be just the thing for him. He is a good man and is in need of friendship to help him feel good about himself, if you understand what I mean."

"I feel good about myself when I do work for you and earn the food you give me. It is better than stealing."

"Then, will you visit him later today?"

"When I have finished helping you and James with the nets." And he immediately set about the task, so familiar to him and the fishing community to which he belonged.

Matt turned to James to raise the topic he'd been mulling over for a few days.

"James, have you noticed how mature we sound when we talk to people?"

James smiled and nodded. "Actually I have, and not for the first time. Once or twice on our previous adventures I noticed that you spoke in a different manner from the way you do at home, and I think the same can be said of me. It must be something to do with the people we become. We've always been fairly influential characters with key roles to play. Here, though, it's a different matter; although people listen to us, we don't seem to be taking a major part."

"What difference does that make?"

"Perhaps we're supposed to be like that, a bit like wise men or something – like Simon, though not quite as influential."

"We know that we assume the form of different people when we go back in time. Do you think we inherit some of their personality and characteristics, then?"

"I do, but not at the expense of our own. I still think and act like James, but sometimes when I speak, it isn't quite how I'd normally say it back home."

"I'm glad you've noticed that, 'cause I was beginning to think I was actually becoming somebody else."

"I s'pose we both are in some respects. After all, surely it's only logical to take on more than a just physical body?"

The Return of Simon and the Tribune

Simon had invited Arte to stay at his home, and now both men had disappeared off somewhere, early in the morning, before the community rose. James had no idea where they'd gone, which he found frustrating as he was favouring the idea that Arte might be the reason for their presence here.

It was another two days before Simon and his guest returned, and the event coincided with Jeremiah being well enough to leave the community building for the first time.

It had been an uneventful couple of days for both the boys, and James, who still remained unsure of their purpose after mulling over every possibility, felt his frustration starting to build.

By contrast, Matt was more bored with the lack of variety in their day-to-day tasks. As he commented to James one morning, "How many more nets can there be to mend? And how do these poor men cope with such a monotonous existence?"

David had developed a tentative friendship with Jeremiah, calling on him several times during his recovery, and Matt had also continued to visit, holding similar deep conversations with him as their first. It was Matt who helped Jeremiah to his feet and waited patiently for the man's shaking form to manage movement, at the effort he put in to even pass hrough the doorway. He took his first few steps into the sunlight, wincing at the brightness that threatened to sear his eyes. The bruising had now faded, but the expanse of the injury was still evident, giving his face a somewhat jaundiced appearance.

One or two passing people smiled at him, congratulating him on his recovery and saying how pleased they were that he was up and about. And many more were amazed at the smiley response they received in return. David appeared and took a position at Jeremiah's other side. He looked up at the big man, telling him to lean on him should he feel the need. Matt couldn't help smiling at this, thinking that if Jeremiah did so, then David would probably collapse under the weight of such a large man.

Guiding him around one or two of the houses, Matt was just about to head back with Jeremiah from his daily quota of exercise, when the cry went up that Simon had returned from his travels. Joined by James, the three of them looked along the beach to see their friend walking calmly towards them, alongside his new companion.

"Who is the man that accompanies Simon?" asked Jeremiah.

"He is the one he left with, a stranger to the village, but not to me," James told him.

"It's odd that Simon didn't introduce him to us all before he went, don't you think?" said Matt in a curious tone, although he guessed at the reason.

"Simon rarely does anything without thought and consideration, so he must have had good reason for it," replied Jeremiah, thoughtfully.

"With any luck we'll all find out, shortly."

Simon walked confidently with his friend through the clusters of people who waited to greet him. He responded warmly to all who spoke to him and waved a greeting to those too far away to hear.

Stopping in front of Jeremiah, he slapped him gently on the arm.

"Shalom, Jeremiah. It is good to see you up and about! I can see you are healing well."

"Shalom, Simon. I have been waiting for the opportunity to talk with you about matters on which only you can advise me. When you are rested from your journey, I would be grateful for a chance to meet with you privately."

"My door is always open to you, Jeremiah – you know that. Shalom, Matt and James. And who is your new friend?" he asked to neither in particular, beaming at the smallest member of the group.

James introduced him. "This is David, a young friend of ours, and helper of fishermen."

"Shalom David. I have seen you before around these parts, but have never learned your name until this moment."

"I have seen you many times before, Simon, for you have given me food even when there has been little to share."

"Will you not introduce us to your travelling companion, Simon?" asked Jeremiah, looking at the hooded figure whose bent head kept his face completely hidden.

"It would be proper to do so, my friends, but I must request we eat and rest first, for our journey has been arduous. Perhaps, Jeremiah, you would join us for a meal after we have rested? I will send someone for you when the time is right. I would like you and James to come, also," he said to Matt.

"Thank you, Simon, I would be happy to accept," replied Jeremiah.

With that, Simon turned and led his companion home, disappearing through the door as the others watched on.

"That is strange behaviour and not what I have come to expect of Simon," said Jeremiah, his curiosity roused. "I need to get off my feet again, too, if I am to be fit enough to attend."

Matt and James helped him back to the community space, leaving him to rest. David stayed with him, in case he needed anything.

Walking back down to the boats, which were now deserted, Matt and James were able to talk in private.

"I just can't work out why we're here, Matt," began James. "We've been here for the best part of two weeks and still nothing appears obvious."

"I know what you mean. I feel it too, but I am beginning to sense that things are being revealed to us in a less obvious way, this time."

"What do you mean?"

"If you think about the people we've been involved with, so far, it has to be something to do with one or other of them."

"Simon, Jeremiah, Jarrod and David," listed James. "Everybody else has had significantly less to do with us than those four."

"I think that we can rule out Jarrod, too."

"What makes you think that?"

"Apart from rescuing him from the sea, there's little to connect us to him apart from casual conversation. I think it's more likely to be one of the others. And David is just a kid; it's unlikely that he has a major role in anything we're here to do."

"That's true, but he's always around us or Jeremiah, and I'm sure that Jeremiah is definitely at the centre of things. I find myself drawn to him for reasons I don't understand. Things just seem to happen when he's about."

"Possibly, but now there's also the stranger Simon has returned with. He might also be the key to something."

"He's hardly a stranger. He revealed a lot to Simon and me that night."

"I guess so, but I have a feeling that there's more to learn – that he's not such an open book as he makes out."

"I feel strongly that he's going to be the reason for our being here, and I'm so convinced that I intend to stay close by."

"I think you're wrong, James, but I understand how you feel. I feel the same way about Jeremiah, so I think I'll stay close to him instead."

"I'm not sure we should separate Matt, we always stay together, work as a team."

"I agree, we do usually but we seem to be thinking a little

differently here. And I know that you are going with your gut, just like me."

"Fair enough. We could both be right, of course. Perhaps we're here for both of them, this time?"

They talked until darkness began to fall, before they made their way back home to wash before going to Simon's.

Later that evening, Simon sent one of his neighbour's children to tell Jeremiah that it was time to eat. The boy helped the injured man to Simon's house, before telling Matt and James, too.

Jeremiah was greeted in the customary manner by Simon and led to a bank of blankets which had been arranged to support his still weakened body. Jeremiah thanked him for his consideration, before his eyes fell on the stranger seated nearby, now without the hood to conceal his face. There was no time to devote any attention to him however, as Matt and James arrived at that point. He greeted them both warmly before turning back to Simon's guest.

Jeremiah studied his face and noted the haircut, knowing immediately why the man had retained the hood earlier on. He was, without doubt, a Roman and someone with power and position, judging by how well-groomed he was. He immediately felt uneasy and worried for the safety of the community.

"Tell me, Simon – why is it that you bring a Roman to shelter in your house?"

"You can feel at ease with this man, Jeremiah. He is not here to hurt you or anyone else. To that, even Matt and James can testify, as this man stopped the soldiers' attack on you."

"He is a soldier?"

"Not just any soldier, Jeremiah – he is, or rather was, a Tribune and one of Caesar's favourites. His name is Artemus Septavia."

"What is he doing here? What does he want with the likes of fishermen who he probably deems are beneath him?"

"For a long time, Artemus has been unhappy about what

he does for a living. He has not been home to see his family in more than five years! His success as a soldier has kept him on the front line, carrying out the Caesar's work, and will continue to do so for many years to come. One day, he came across a gathering of people listening to the Rabbi preaching. He was moved by what the Rabbi taught and wished to learn more, until he found out that the Rabbi was teaching that there is only one true God. To the Roman people this is sacrilege and he ordered the meeting to be broken up."

Artemus took over the story...

"I travelled for many days afterwards with troubling thoughts. My own teachings could not accept such things, for it is against everything I have ever believed in, and yet I somehow knew that this Rabbi was speaking the truth. I could not doubt the sincerity of his words. Then, after dwelling on this for many weeks, I decided to seek out the Rabbi again. As I did not know where to find him, someone suggested I talk to Simon, who is a friend of his. So I sought him out; Simon took me to see the Rabbi and I was finally able to talk with him."

"What did you learn, Roman?" pressed Jeremiah.

"I learned how to find peace of mind when I prayed with him, and I learned the commandments that he lives his life by. I cannot return to my old life in the army but, because of this, I risk my life and will be branded a traitor. So I can never return home to my wife and the child I have yet to see."

"If you are not found, then you cannot be branded anything. They might perhaps conclude that you have succumbed to robbers and been murdered."

"If I am presumed dead, at least my family would not be disgraced at the memory of me nor would they be stripped of their lands and possessions.

"For now, I am too easily recognised; the style of my hair is uniquely Roman, for one thing. It is, after all, how you recognised me, isn't it?"

Jeremiah nodded and asked a simple question.

"Do you still have peace in your head and your heart?"

"I do, and I recognise it as a lasting peace. Why do you ask?"

"I have been searching for peace such as this for many years, and until now, did not know where to look for it. I was meaning to talk to Simon about this tonight, but it appears that it is no longer necessary."

"Do you believe, as Simon does, in the one God, Jeremiah?

"I have not believed in any God for a long, long time, but the peace such belief offers is what I seek once more."

"It would be my pleasure to help you achieve that, Jeremiah," offered Simon.

"Thank you, my friend, but you must know that it is not safe here for the Tribune. All it would take is one sighting, one person to talk out of place and he will be taken away for punishment and certain death."

"For now I have to take that chance, but I do know that the army garrison is due to move further west of its current position, about one hundred leagues, I believe. If I can avoid discovery until it has left, then I will have a chance of freedom and peace. I will never have to lift a sword again to take a human life. There is one other around here who has seen me. It is a boy who goes by the name of Michael. Do you know of him? He has been kind and helpful to me."

Jeremiah shook his head.

"There are many children around here and most do not use a name."

"David might know him," said James, speaking for the first time.

"I could ask him. Does he know your name?" he asked smiling.

"He calls me Arte."

They talked well into the night before sleep finally caught up with them. Matt and James said little, but listened carefully to everything the soldier and Jeremiah discussed. They both noticed that Simon, too, said very little, preferring to allow the first shoots of friendship to grow between Arte and Jeremiah. Both boys left with the feeling that their immediate future definitely involved these two men in some way.

In the morning, Jeremiah and Matt set off for the hills with

David to find Michael and tell him never to mention Arte to anybody, while Simon went to find James with the intention of seeking his help to protect Artemus.

Rampage

For the meantime, Simon had decided that the Tribune's identity was to be kept from the rest of the village. When James asked why nobody else was to be entrusted with the news, he was told emphatically that it was too much to expect the average person to conceal, should they or their families ever be threatened.

James suggested that, as the Tribune's presence here was so risky, he should perhaps be taken to another place to hide. Although Simon hadn't considered that option, he agreed that it made sense. The boy, David, would be able to act as a runner between them.

"And now, we just need a safe place to hide him," continued Simon, thinking hard.

It was the Tribune himself who came up with an idea.

"While I was waiting on the hillside, the child named Michael was tending my needs. He told me about some caves where homeless children like him spend their time during the winter months. It's close to a leper colony and is rarely visited by anyone who isn't sick with the disease. Perhaps you know where he means?"

"I know the place! It's a fair walk down the coast, but it would make an ideal hiding place. The afflicted use only part of the cave system there and leave the rest unoccupied for others, should they need it, such as the homeless children.

Even in the midst of their suffering, they find kindness in their hearts for others," replied Simon, liking the idea more and more."

"Jeremiah would show me the way, would he not?" the Tribune asked Simon.

"I am sure he would, and perhaps Matthew and James would accompany you to ensure your safety?"

James nodded. "We'd be pleased to help you get set up. In fact, it would be easier and safer if we go by boat. We could travel on the night tide and return the following day. Nobody would see where we went or where we stopped."

"And what reason could you give those who question you when you get back?" asked Simon.

"Well, the catches have been poor lately; I could stop at the next village and ask how their fishing has been. When I return, it will sound like I was trying to get information about where to fish," James said. "Nobody will know I had a second reason for my trip."

"I think your plan could work. I will need to gather some simple supplies and food for Arte's stay. Perhaps David can take them covertly down to your boat. Nobody takes much notice of the boys who run around the village all day. You will go tonight, yes?"

James nodded and wandered down to the boats to tell Matt what they had decided. Surprisingly, Jeremiah was already at the boat, chatting away to Matt, much as he often did himself. When he told them of the plan, Jeremiah suggested they tow his own small craft behind their boat when they left, and disappeared off to fetch it.

The boat he returned with was smaller and narrower. Inside there was little room, but folded nets filled one end and a pair of oars lay down the remaining length.

"Do you think we're looking at the world's oldest canoe?" asked Matt with a grin.

"Native peoples have been using canoes for thousands of years so I very much doubt it! Anyway, I'm not even sure if it is a canoe."

"I wonder why he wants to take it with us," said Matt, changing the subject.

"I bet he's going to teach the Tribune how to use it, so that he can catch his own food," answered James. "What a good idea!"

During the hottest part of the day, the drowsy peace was interrupted by the sound of screams and shouting. Many of the community rushed towards the general direction of the ruckus.

"What is it?" Jeremiah asked a man a few paces ahead of him.

"The Roman soldiers have returned and they're ransacking one of the houses," he replied, his voice betraying the fear he felt. "There were about ten soldiers and their leader, this time – they were searching for something."

Simon approached the Decanus. "Whatever is it that you seek, can it not be done in a more civilised manner?" he asked, receiving a blow for his perceived rudeness.

"You insolent dog! How dare you question me?"

"I wish only to help you in your quest," persisted Simon, ignoring the pain to his cheek bone.

"Where are all the children? The ones who have no family?"

"They do not stay among us; they just appear after each fishing trip, begging for a few fish to eat."

"I do not believe you. Kneel down before me, you dog, because if I find a single child who is not related to a fisherman, I am going to whip you to death for lying."

"I will sit for you, but I will kneel only for God."

Simon received two more blows from the Decanus that made his knees buckle. He slumped to the ground, immediately rising unsteadily to his feet again, his vision swimming alarmingly, just as a beautifully made multi-coloured blanket seemed to come flying out of the nearest house. It distracted the Decanus sufficiently who bent to pick it up and examine it more closely, before moving off, issuing further orders to his men.

The search continued and no house was left untouched. Children stood clinging to their mothers' long robes, wailing piteously; goats and chickens scattered in alarm as they were chased from buildings. The violence was completely needless, but the frenzied soldiers were in battle-mode and continued their rampage throughout the village.

Simon held his breath while his own house and James' were searched, feeling highly relieved when the soldiers came out again without either the Tribune or David. He wondered where they had gone to hide.

Matt and James, angry at this treatment of the people, both recognised the leader as the soldier they had seen up on the mountainside with the whip so soon after their arrival. Suggesting James follow his lead, Matt moved amongst the fishermen, whispering briefly in their ears and receiving nods of confirmation in return.

Simon watched as, apparently unprompted, something strange began to occur. At first, so slowly that the soldiers were unaware it was happening, the fishermen had formed a rough circle around them. Then, almost casually, they began moving towards them from all directions, penning them in. There were about thirty fishermen altogether, more than a match for just ten soldiers – if they had also been armed.

Matt and James slipped away from the circle, taking up position alongside Simon. As the soldiers searched the last few houses, the circle of fishermen grew tighter, until they were two deep. Still in their heightened state, the soldiers failed to notice. As they emerged from the final two houses, again without success, their fervour began to dissipate and they suddenly noticed that they were completely surrounded.

"It would appear that your men are surrounded, which leaves you isolated and alone," stated Simon, facing the Decanus once more.

"You are all but isolated too, and I am the one with the sword," he declared angrily, sneering at Matt and James.

They said nothing but held their ground, poised and ready,

in case the Roman made a move toward Simon.

"Look again, Decanus and you will see that, indeed, I am not alone!"

As he said this, the women of the village, organised by Martha, stepped forward and surrounded the man.

"You will pay dearly for this lack of respect," he seethed.

"Have I not already paid at the expense of your blows? Have the people of this village not already paid with the destruction of their property? I think you have seen that there are no children here, and that this has all been for nothing! It is time for you to leave."

Despite the fact that Simon was unarmed, the Decanus felt threatened. He was becoming increasingly uncomfortable with the man who stood before him with no fear on his face, and who was as calm as the sea on a windless day. His men were experiencing similar feelings, despite having the advantage of weapons in their hands.

The Decanus shouted an order and the men tried, unsuccessfully at first, to form a two-man file. The second barked order encouraged them to stride forward and a gap in the circle of fishermen opened obligingly.

"We will meet again, fisherman," promised the Decanus, as he turned away, marching to the front of his men.

Simon did not reply, but smiled at the women who had come to his side, and then at the men who had acted in such a peaceful manner and secured the community's safety.

Everybody assisted in clearing up the mess the soldiers had caused. Their initial silence gradually gave way to cautious laughter – they felt relief and pride at the thought of their little victory over the Roman soldiers.

Both James and Matt were looking forward to the trip that night and relished the break in the monotony of their routine. There was little to do between fishing trips after the nets had been repaired. The fishermen spent most of this time with their families, but those without families hung around in small groups playing games or talking. The two of them were not used to such a sedate pace of life and found it very challenging.

After the evening meal, and when the darkness was complete, a small band of men made their way individually down to James' boat. Simon walked down with the Tribune, talking quietly with him about the day's events. The Tribune warned Simon about the evil nature of the Decanus and advised him to be very wary of the soldier, should he meet him again.

As the boat was launched, Simon waved them off and the group of four men and a child sailed out into the darkness.

Both James and Matt felt uneasy travelling the sea at night, but they kept close to the shoreline where they could just make out the white of the breaking waves. With no moon, conditions were perfect to conceal their operation. But as they had no knowledge of those waters, they still had to take care for there might be tidal rips or rocks below the surface. The wind, little more than a breeze, barely filled the sails, making progress frustratingly slow.

There had been little conversation as sound travels easily over still, quiet waters, but Jeremiah's voice broke the silence again.

"David and I will not be coming back with you, Matt. It is my desire to stay for a while with Arte and teach him to fish. I also wish to find wood in the locality that I might use to build another boat like this one."

"I had forgotten that you can build boats, Jeremiah," said James.

"Surely you have not forgotten that I built this very boat, albeit for your father, as well as most of the fleet we have left behind."

"It has been a while since you practised the skill though, Jeremiah."

"It has been too long, James, and indeed I have all but forgotten the satisfaction my trade used to bring me each day as I laboured with the wood."

"I hope that when you resume building, that familiar

feeling returns."

"Thank you, my friend, already the anticipation of it pleases me."

The Storm

It had been a few days since Matt and James had left Jeremiah, David and the Tribune on the beach near the caves. They had landed further along the coast than necessary, but that was to ensure they did not meet those living in the caves who suffered from leprosy. They could not risk anyone knowing their intentions. Matt and James both wished they could have done something for the sick, but they didn't know what they would be able to do to help.

The fleet had been fishing twice in the past three days with the resulting catches too small to feed the village – Simon was particularly worried, as the responsibility he assumed for the community lay heavy with him. Since the enormous catch they had achieved on the day of Jarrod's accident, little had been caught and with the leaner months of late autumn approaching, the need to start drying fish for the winter was paramount.

News of a meeting for the fishermen, called by Simon, reached Matt and James via Martha, who had taken it upon herself to regularly check on their welfare since Matt had saved Jarrod's life.

"What's the meeting about, Martha?" asked James, his interest piqued.

"Simon didn't say, but I would think that it is to do with the poor catches we have been experiencing."

Matt voiced his thoughts. "He must have a plan or something, maybe he's going to suggest going farther out to sea."

"That has been tried in the past, but not always with a significant improvement in the catch. It is also risky for the men, since the water is deeper and the swells are greater. Whatever he is thinking, he hasn't shared with anyone yet, not even Jarrod."

"Thanks for bringing the news, Martha, we will be along shortly."

"The meeting is at our house, and I have made soup to share."

"I've tried your soup before, Martha, and I certainly won't pass up an opportunity for another helping," said Matt smiling.

Martha turned away quickly, to prevent Matt seeing the blush that coloured her cheeks at his compliment.

A few minutes later, the two of them strolled over to Jarrod's house to find that they were among the last to arrive. With so many fishermen packed into the small space, there was little room to sit, but nobody complained and each man was given a small bowl of delicious soup. Almost immediately after their arrival, the final members of the fleet squeezed through the doorway, and Simon raised his hand for quiet.

"Shalom, my friends! Now we have eaten, we have serious matters to discuss. The scarcity of fish that has recently stricken our community has robbed us of many weeks' preparation for the harsher winter months. It is time to take more desperate measures to secure the food we need for our stores. In times past, when faced with a similar shortage, we have sailed farther out into deeper, more treacherous waters to fish. As you know only too well, this has had very mixed results, often not worth the time or effort we put in, not to mention the danger and frequency of the autumnal storms. This time, however, we will try something different. I suggest that we all travel in different directions and scour the sea to find the whereabouts of the great shoals of fish. We will sail for one day out and one day back. Each of us will fish during that time and whoever is the most successful will lead the fleet to that site when we have all returned."

"This is not the safest way to travel, Simon. Would it not be better if the fleet went out in pairs?" It was an older fisherman who spoke.

"Normally, I would agree with you, Zachariah, but every day we are forced to search is a day we are not able to prepare for the winter."

Zachariah nodded his agreement.

Another spoke up. "Is there to be a pattern to the areas we search or is it to be completely random?"

"Each of us has fished alone at different times, in preferred areas that we visit time and time again. It is the right time for us to use our individual knowledge and experience for the good of the whole community."

"When will we go?"

"I can go now!" called one fisherman.

"The tide is not yet full."

"We can launch without waiting for the tide – it is harder work but it can be done."

The meeting broke up and the fishermen went to their boats to make their preparations. Matt and James were already prepared and quickly loaded food and water onto the boat. They signalled some of the others to assist them with the launch and noticed that Simon was missing from the group.

"Where is Simon?" asked James.

"He has gone to fetch another," came the mysterious reply from one of the fishermen.

"If you see him tell, him that we travel west of our community."

"I will do so, and may your nets bulge with fish, James."

"Yours also, my friend."

The wind was already fresh and as they raised their sail, they felt its strength. The little craft quickly picked up speed and skipped across the waves. Spray from the deepening swells constantly drenched their bodies, making the mild temperatures seem a lot colder. Salt from the spray remained on their clothes and skin long after the moisture had evaporated, forming a thin layer almost like flour.

"How far should we go before we start fishing, James?"

"I don't think we should fish at all until we see obvious signs of fish."

"What do you mean?"

"If we start spreading our nets randomly, the likelihood of catching something is remote and, what's worse, we'd exhaust ourselves quickly with the effort involved. We need to watch for signs such as bird activity on the water. If the fish come near enough to the surface, they attract the seabirds. When we see that happening, we'll know it's the right place to cast our nets."

"What if we don't see any birds?"

"Then we don't fish until we are on the way home when we can afford to use all our strength and effort."

"It makes sense, I s'pose, but I don't feel at all confident. The wind's increasing and the swells are deepening, and if the conditions get any worse we may spend most of our time hanging on for dear life."

"If it gets much worse, we're going to turn round and head back. Although we always seem to know what to do, we just don't have enough experience of rough conditions to take any unnecessary chances."

Conditions continued to deteriorate, almost by the minute, as the wind kept building. The sun and then the sky disappeared behind an evil-looking mass of dark grey cumulous clouds. The wind began to hum around the top of the mast, a wailing hum that altered in pitch and cried like a banshee. And then the rain started, falling heavily, stinging their exposed skin with the sheer force, as it quickly washed away the itchy salt residue. They were forced to start bailing as the water rapidly built up in the bottom of their craft. Despite their best efforts, they were unable to stem the rising waters.

"I'm going to try and turn the boat around. It's going to

get a little hairy when we come sideways on to the wind," shouted James, as loudly as he could. His voice was carried away on another severe gust.

"Lower the sail, James! We don't stand a chance with that up, we'll capsize."

"You lower it, Matt. I'm going to start the turn, the second it's down."

Matt did as he was told and instantly the speed bled off the boat. The violent rocking as the craft ran up and down the swells, increased as it began to turn, coming broadside on to the wind and waves.

"Hang on, Matt," cried James halfway through the 180-degree turn, seeing a huge wave bearing down on them. Matt saw it too and gripped the mast by locking his arms around it. He closed his eyes just as the massive breaker was about to crash down on top of them.

James, still trying to steer, said a silent, desperate prayer as he looked certain death in the face.

Suddenly, as if by magic, a strong gust of wind from the opposite direction hit the side of the vessel, pushing it the remainder of the turn. Instead of the wave crashing down onto them, it lifted them up as it passed beneath them and continued onwards, caught in the constant chase of the wave in front of it.

James uncharacteristically whooped and laughed almost maniacally as relief flooded in and the fear left his body. With all his senses tingling, he realised he had just cheated death.

Matt opened his eyes, and on registering that the wave had passed by, he too laughed out loud with his friend as the boat now rode with the waves, back in the direction they had come.

As the euphoria gradually left them, they felt drained and exhausted. Matt raised the sail until just half of it unfolded, before tying it off. It was held now by the thicker end of the mast with no pressure applied to the top and thinner end, which meant less chance of snapping the mast in half.

"We rode our luck close to the edge just then," Matt

shouted over at James.

"Tell me something I don't know already," he replied and turned away, suddenly embarrassed by his uncontrolled release of emotion.

In a single instant, the wind stopped, the rain ceased and the huge swells flattened before their eyes. The clouds disappeared, the sun broke through and blue sky appeared once more. In a few blinks of the eye, it was as if the storm had been but a figment of their imaginations.

The two boys looked at each other incredulously.

"Did we just dream all that?" asked Matt.

"I have the bruises to show that we didn't."

"This is a bit weird. I know storms can pass quickly and the wind cease suddenly, but I would have thought the sea would take hours to calm after a storm like that."

"Did you see what happened to the clouds?"

"What do you mean? That they just disappeared?"

"They seemed to swirl and disappear at a central point, a bit like a fluid down a drain, only this was sort of upside down."

"Well, *whatever* just happened, I am very glad it did! I don't think we would have lasted much longer."

"I hope the rest of the fleet is ok."

"Me too, buddy, me too."

"Hey! What's that over there?" cried Matt, with sudden urgency.

"That, my friend, is the sign we've been looking for! Bird activity like that means fish, and close to the surface, too. Raise the sail, we're going fishing!"

Five minutes later, the boys were lowering their nets into the sea. James steered the boat in a circle so that the net followed suit. There were so many seabirds diving around them that both of them had to duck as they whistled past their heads before entering the water, perfectly streamlined. Fish began to jump out of the water in their thousands and James stared open-mouthed at them in amazement.

"If only the rest of the fleet were here!" cried Matt, as he started to heave on the net to pull it in.

It took all their strength to retrieve the net bulging with fish and haul it on board the boat.

"We are going to be in danger of sinking, if the nets are this full the entire way along."

"If we have to, we can always put some back. There'd be little point in doing all this work, just to sink!" replied Matt with a laugh.

"If it stays calm we should be alright, so long as it doesn't take too long to bring the catch home."

"It would be a good idea to drop some off to Jeremiah en route. We've surely gone up the coast far enough to pass the caves, if we head directly towards land."

"Let's do it then! We'll head back as soon as we've retrieved the nets."

12

The Christian Thing to Do

Without much of a breeze, and with a full load of fish, progress back to land was slow. Even with a full spread of sail to catch the breeze, it barely fluttered. The currents pushed them along though, and after several hours, the boat finally reached the shelf that inclined steeply to the shallows and the approaching shoreline.

Three figures stood on the beach, waving in recognition at the vessel and the silhouettes who stood on it. Two men and a child! James and Matt recognised them, waving in return. Then, moments later, the boat slowed to a stop, the shallow keel burying itself in the sand and anchoring the boat against the now ebbing tide.

"Shalom, James! Shalom, Matthew! By the look of your success, God has seriously blessed your nets," Jeremiah said, with a grin that showed his delight at the sight of all the fish.

"Shalom! We were on our way back to the village but had so many fish, we wondered if you would like some," offered James.

The Tribune stepped forward to inspect the boat and the catch.

"Shalom, my friends! It is good to see you again and we would be pleased to relieve you of some of the fish. But in truth, we would like more than you might be prepared to give," he said, enigmatically.

Matt looked at him curiously. "Why would that be, Tribune?"

"Please do not call me that any more, Matthew. I am no longer a Tribune. I answer only to Artemus now or Arte, for short. Not too far down the beach are some caves that belong to a group of people suffering from leprosy. They survive on food that is sent in by relatives, but it is meagre pickings. Even in their hunger and poor health, they share whatever is sent without reservation, like the true Christians they have become. A fair percentage of the catch you have here would be sufficient to see them through the leaner of the winter months, if the catch was dried. Would you be prepared to help them?"

"I am uncertain at the moment whether any more of our boats have experienced the same success as ours, Arte, as we all fished independently—"

"Things must have been desperate to make the fleet split like that. The last time I remember that happening was at least ten years ago," interrupted Jeremiah.

"The fishing has been poor lately and Simon was concerned that we had nothing put aside for the coming season, so he suggested that we split up to try to locate the shoals."

"It is a good strategy, but sometimes even when fish are located, by the time the rest of the fleet returns to the spot, they have already moved on."

"How much fish do these people need, Arte?"

"There are at least thirty living there, so as much as you can spare; they are far worse off than those at our village."

"If that is the case then they must have it, but how can we get it to them?"

"You will need to sail down the coast and take it to them, for we do not have any other way of transporting it. Will you do that for them, James?"

"Of course we will, but we could use some help unloading it."

"I will come with you and, when we have done the work, I can walk back along the shoreline."

"We're coming too," said Jeremiah, speaking for David too.

"Will you join us in a meal before we go? David will stay to guard the catch from the gulls that threaten it."

"That would be very welcome, thank you. The food we took with us was spoilt by sea water during the storm – we haven't eaten since we left the village."

The four of them walked up the sandy incline leading to a cliff face nearly a hundred metres high. To their left were several large caves above the high tide line. Jeremiah strode ahead of the others showing the direction of the cave they now called home. It was riddled with tunnels that ran from a central space in several directions. Just inside the entrance, carefully laid out, were timbers in the rough shape of a new boat, which Jeremiah had started working on.

Inside one of the tunnels only a few metres in length, Jeremiah led them into a circular living area that opened out from it. A small fire crackled, over which a pot of something bubbled away invitingly, filling the space with a delicious aroma. He indicated for Matt and James to sit and ladled some of the stew into wooden bowls for them.

"Arte went to see the Rabbi with Simon to get some advice because of his desire to leave the Roman army. It was the Rabbi's idea for us to come to this particular section of caves. There is little chance of being discovered, and he told him that if he wanted to become a true Christian, then he would need to live his life in the service of others. He must have known that the Lepers were here, and that they needed help," Jeremiah said, starting up the conversation.

"If this is what you want, Arte, then it is truly a good thing that you do. The lepers may be ill and contagious, but they are still human beings," James offered.

"I am letting my hair and beard grow, so that I might one day pass as one of you, but it will take time. Until then, I will remain here and do whatever I can to help these poor wretches."

"What about your wife and child back in Rome?"

"I fear they are lost to me, at least for the time being, but who knows what might happen with the passing of time."

"And what about you, Jeremiah?" asked Matt.

"I have also spoken to the Rabbi who told me that I must do God's work too, but that I must seek this work for myself. He said I will know what I am to do when I am faced with it. I have to admit that I have found this frustrating and, to be quite honest, I am not the world's most patient man," he smiled, apologetically.

"Do you think your work is to be here with Arte?" asked James.

"I am thinking that it might not be. I have prayed on the matter and, of course, I will help Arte wherever I can, but if my destiny is not here, then I must return to the village to see if it lies there instead. Perhaps I shall speak to the Rabbi again on the matter. If it is alright with you, I would like to come back with you for a few days. The journey back here is simple enough along the shoreline."

"You are welcome, Jeremiah, but what of the boy?"

"David is very much his own person, and has assisted us in doing God's work with the lepers. The decision should be his to make. He is comfortable with both Arte and me, as he is also with Matthew. He knows that we would all care for him, whatever he decides, but my belief is that he will go wherever he thinks he is needed the most."

With the meal finished, they headed down to the boat, where David was patiently waiting for them. He gratefully took the bowl of food that Arte had carried down for him, eating it with relish, while Jeremiah told him of their plans. The boy decided to stay with Arte at the caves, and not return to the village just yet. He told Matt that there was a lot of work still to do with the construction of the boat and, though he and Arte did not have Jeremiah's building skills, they could at least cut and split the timber into lengths, which he could work with when he returned.

They all pushed the boat back down into the sea, and climbed aboard to head up the coast. They hugged the shoreline closely, not straying into water more than two fathoms deep, and arrived in front of the lepers' caves in less than half an hour. Arte jumped off the boat, even before it came to a stop, and ran up the beach. He stood in front of the caves shouting instructions that those on the boat could not hear. When he turned and came back, people started to appear at the entrances to the caves, carrying baskets with which to load with fish.

"They will not come any closer to us. After we have unloaded the fish onto the beach and left, they will come to collect them. They have no desire to pass on the disease to anybody," explained Arte.

It took them a long time to unload half of the bountiful catch onto the beach but, even then, Matt asked Arte if he thought it was enough.

"It is enough, of that I am sure. I am forever in your debt for this display of kindness and mercy," Arte told them gratefully. "

"Jeremiah, do you still wish to return to the village?" James asked

"I do, but I do not think the timing is right. There is so much to do here."

"Why don't you go back with Matthew, and I will stay with Arte and do some of the work you intended for yourself?"

Matt moved away slightly, catching James' eye as he did so. James understood the gesture and followed his friend.

"We shouldn't separate James, we are better and safer as a pair. I don't like this!"

"Don't be silly, Matt. We know that everything seems to hinge around Arte and Jeremiah, so we need to stay close to them. And you get on better with Jeremiah while I seem to have hit it off ok with Arte."

"Matt's eyes flashed for a moment. "I'm *not* being silly, far from it! Besides, *you* haven't exactly been acting like your normal self since we've been here."

"I told you why acted like I did, get over it! This has been a strange adventure for both of us, and maybe it calls for a change in approach."

Matt was both surprised and angered at the way James dismissed his views. He bit his tongue and walked away, peevishly kicking at the sand. They would talk again about this, but now was not the time.

James returned to Jeremiah and Arte.

"It's settled then. I will stay until you return, Jeremiah."

David helped James and Arte push the boat, releasing it from the grip of the sand. The three began to walk back in the direction of Arte's cave, turning their heads to watch the people of the colony come down and begin loading their baskets with the unexpected windfall. Several raised their arms in thanks, to the two in the boat who responded in kind.

Theirs was the last boat to return home. Everyone else had returned hours ago, each with a similar haul of fish.

One or two of the fishermen teased Matt for only having half a boatload of fish, but Jeremiah soon put paid to that by threatening to wrestle each of them into an apology. The teasing was good-natured, as was Jeremiah's rebuke, and before long, he had explained to the villagers the reason why the boat was only half full.

Making his appearance soon after, Simon smiled at Jeremiah and an exhausted-looking Matt.

"It would seem that your journey has been eventful and that you have been more than generous with your bounty. It is indeed a good thing that you have done today. Perhaps we could discuss the events at a later time, but I suspect that, for now, you need to rest."

"Rest is my number one priority as I have had none since we left," answered Matt tiredly. "But, afterwards, I would welcome the chance to talk."

"Perhaps I might take the opportunity to discuss a matter with you," suggested Jeremiah.

"Gladly! You know that my door is always open to you."

Many members of the community turned out to help Matt and Jeremiah unload the catch. The women took it away in baskets to gut and clean, while the men laid the nets out on the beach to dry. The mast was lowered, the boat turned onto its side and the inside of the boat cleaned of the fishy detritus by a procession of eager children who collected water from the sea for the task.

Martha insisted Matt went home to rest, saying that others would help take care of what was needed.

Agreeing, he lumbered off, sighing with relief as he lay back on his bed and closed his eyes. He did not wake until dawn the following morning and, as he stretched and watched the sun come up through the small window, he couldn't help wondering what the new day would bring.

Marathon Runner

Making his way towards Jeremiah's abode, Matt was surprised to learn that he'd left the village with Simon; neither had mentioned any plans for a trip. He guessed it was to see the Rabbi, but he was secretly disappointed that the man he had been hoping to spend some time with had chosen to leave him behind.

All the men of the village were tending to the harvest today and he sought out Martha and Jarrod to work with. The crop yield was not particularly fruitful this year, especially as the soil conditions around the village were particularly dry and sandy. Nothing was left behind, however, as they systematically cleared all the plants from the earth.

On the morning of the third day of Simon and Jeremiah's absence, Matt was once again contemplating the purpose of his visit to this place and time. He thought about the things that he and James had already played a part in, but was still trying to find a bigger reason for their presence.

"There has to be more to it than this. Every time we've gone through the portal, we've been involved in serious, life-and-death adventures; here, it's do something one day, then nothing for the next three or four," he said aloud, voicing his frustration. Fortunately, there was nobody in earshot to overhear his ponderings.

"Maybe that is our role here? Maybe our small contributions

are helping some bigger picture that we just can't see right now. I have to be honest, I'm starting to get pretty bored," he continued out loud in the same manner, almost as if he were talking to James.

"There has to be more to come, but I must try to think rationally. We're so far back in time that nothing happens particularly quickly. Apart from the odd horse and donkey, all travel is by foot; news is by word of mouth and subject to the interpretations of the tellers and, in turn, who they choose to tell it to. It's a bit like the traditional tales we used to do at school in Literacy class, where there are many variations on a single theme. Still, if nothing happens in the next few days, then I'll suggest to James that we go back."

He felt better for airing his views, even if it had only been to himself! Almost as he finished speaking, a cry went up from a man pointing in the direction of the beach at a small figure running towards them – it was David.

"If he's run all the way at that pace, then something is definitely wrong," said Matt, anxiously.

Jarrod and Matt started to run towards the small boy who collapsed on the sand in front of them. David was panting furiously and his chest rose and fell as he gasped for air. There was little perspiration on him and Matt realised that he was probably dehydrated. Some of the workouts he and James had endured pre-season had pushed them to their limit and left them with severe headaches, before they learned that they needed to drink more water during their training.

"Jarrod, fetch some water," ordered Matt, and his friend dashed back up the beach to the nearest house.

Matt spoke calm words of reassurance as he raised the boy's head, looking into fear-filled eyes. Seeing his friend's face above him, the boy struggled to speak, but the saliva had long since dried and his tongue seemed stuck to the roof of his mouth.

Returning with the water, Jarrod gently trickled a little into the boy's mouth as a small crowd gathered to see what was going on. David tried to gulp down mouthfuls of the liquid, but Matt held him back and told him to sip it slowly. Even the slow trickle brought about an amazing transition in the boy's demeanour and his strength flowed back as the water revived him.

"Have you run all the way back from the caves, David?"

"Yes! There are soldiers, many of them, in the village further on from the caves. They are torturing and killing people there and have threatened to seek out and burn the lepers in their caves. I am worried for Arte because he has said that he will no longer fight with the sword. If they find him, he will not protect himself."

A tear fell from his eye.

"I did not know what to do, and you and Jeremiah had not returned," he continued, miserably.

"But I have returned, boy!" A deep voice penetrated the murmur of the small crowd gathered around the boy.

As the realisation hit him, David struggled to his feet. Jeremiah's great frame bent down, his thick arms gathering the boy up effortlessly as he engulfed him in a hug.

"Let us take him to your house, Matthew, so that we can get the full story in private." They returned to the village, with David clinging to his giant friend.

Back at the house, Jeremiah sat down on a wooden bench, placing David on his lap.

"Now, boy, tell me all that has been happening."

David described how the soldiers came to the village, demanding food and wine; how they got drunk, picking on some of the locals until they went too far and actually killed a man for sport. He told how he had hidden in the village, listening to them plotting their next mission, which was to clear the settlements of lepers; how he'd watch them beat a woman, almost to death, just to find out the location of the caves; and then he had sneaked back to Arte in the depths of the night.

Arte had asked him to run and find Jeremiah and then to collect a pack of goods that he'd hidden in a particular tree.

The final instruction had been not to come back until he had found this pack.

"Do you know what is in it?" asked Matt.

David shook his head.

"I don't think anything can protect the lepers or Arte from those soldiers, if they find him."

"I'm not sure they'll even have to find him, for he will go to them, James," said Jeremiah, ruefully.

"Not without his pack. Whatever is in it must be really important to him. I think he'll wait for David to return with it," responded Matt. "Do you have any idea what we could do, Jeremiah?"

"The only thing that would deter the soldiers from fighting would be to outnumber them. What if we took the whole community up there on the boats, men and women both?"

"What good would that do without weapons? They're like madmen, in their frenzy. We'd be slaughtered."

"What if we were all armed with the tools we use in the fields?"

"They'd be no match against the soldiers' swords," Matt pointed out.

"The idea would not be to fight but to intimidate. After what David has told us about the happenings in that village, I think we could swell our numbers even more. We could ask some of them to join us."

"Where is Simon, Jeremiah? I'd like to hear what he thinks about all of this."

"He is with the Rabbi and will not be back for some days."

"Then we should not delay further. We need to organise an emergency meeting with the community right now!"

Jeremiah and Matt sent word of the meeting and, immediately, people started to gather at the community dwelling. They were told about the village which the soldiers were currently occupying and of the lepers' plight. It didn't take long before a unanimous decision had been reached to go to their aid.

With the decision made, people began to leave, either to

collect the tools they'd need or to prepare the boats. A few elderly members of the community stayed behind to watch over the children.

David, having disappeared for a short time, turned up with a neatly tied bundle on his back. Nobody suggested that he stay behind, knowing it was pointless, as he refused to leave Jeremiah's side.

Everyone piled into the boats. With the wind in their favour, they quickly got underway. In less than two hours the boats were hauled up along the beach, above the high tide line.

A lone figure walked towards them, greeting Jeremiah and Matt by name. Arte's black beard and hair had grown a little longer and more tousled, with tight curls becoming evident. His exposed skin was heavily tanned and he no longer looked like the Roman soldier he had been. Indeed, many of the community did not recognise him. As some slowly came aware who he was, his very presence spread a wave of distrust and fear.

Jeremiah, sensing the feeling of disquiet, had to work hard at convincing the group that this was a good man who now sought a righteous path in life and who was here to help the poor lepers, just as they were.

Once the mutterings from the group had subsided, Matt was finally able to ask the question that had been on his mind from his first moment ashore.

"Where is James?"

"Right now, he's in the village where the soldiers are. He is safe and has somewhere to hide, but he's set himself the task of spying on them so that we will have ample warning when they finally make their move against the lepers.

Matt nodded. Disappointment crept through him at the way James had acted without discussing it first with him. He could have, *should have* waited. Now he was alone in a very dangerous situation and Matt didn't even know how to get to him.

Since their arrival at the lepers' caves, none of the

inhabitants had made themselves visible to the group and, to everyone's surprise and horror, Arte and Jeremiah walked up to one of the caves, calling for an audience. A woman appeared, sitting downwind of the two men but, although the community listened closely, none could hear the conversation taking place. As she disappeared back into the cave, the two men returned.

David had been sent to the village to relieve James. He travelled with Andrew, who was to spread the news of their arrival with two of the village elders and share their plans to banish the soldiers.

When Andrew returned later that evening, he told the news they had all been dreading; that there were about sixty soldiers, each group of ten led by a Decanus; and that the one in overall charge was none other than Lucius Asina, the soldier who had threatened them and struck Simon so viciously.

The soldiers had already killed several people and were now entertaining themselves torturing some poor unfortunates. Their imminent arrival at the leper colony was scheduled for midday, the following day. That didn't leave much time for preparations.

When asked about James, Andrew said that he insisted on staying in the village to see how things progressed.

Matt suggested that everybody head to Arte's caves where they would be safe and comfortable for the night, and from where they would coordinate their appearance at the lepers' caves with the arrival of the soldiers.

Jeremiah headed inland to hide, waiting for the soldiers to move out. He would run back to warn the community when to start on their way the next morning. From an aerial perspective, the rival forces would be travelling together, one above the cliffs and one below, each hidden from the other until the soldiers descended the cliffs for the caves.

There was little to do now, except eat and enjoy the community feeling filling the tight space that evening. Matt sat with Jarrod and Martha, who cooked for him. They swapped stories in the age-old tradition of sharing history, though Matt's stories were improvised and adapted on the spot. He couldn't allow them to think there was anything at all strange about his background.

Arte organised watchers along the beach in shifts throughout the night, though he didn't anticipate them seeing anything untoward.

The community gradually went to sleep at the mouths of the caves, and under the stars that blossomed in their millions. It wasn't the most restful sleep for many, but there was comfort to be drawn from the safety of their numbers.

In the morning, and after a quick early meal, preparations would be made to confront the Romans, after which the group would wait the long, lonely wait of all soldiers about to head into battle. Fear and uncertainty pervaded the atmosphere and many would doubt the wisdom of their actions, though none would show signs of a weakened resolve. Banter, and even laughter, would eventually break out to rally themselves for the inevitable conclusion of what they were about to do. And Matt, from a time two thousand years distant, would feel exactly the same.

Captured

In his concealed position, James had crouched for far too long. He could no longer feel his legs and knew that he would need to move soon to allow the blood to flow through them once more. The bush he had all but buried himself in was thick and thorny, and his body carried fresh lacerations as testament to its protective armour. He had been observing the soldiers running riot for some time now; destroying the villagers' meagre possessions in an almost infantile, tantrum-like manner. Watching their general brutality with distaste, he looked on with absolute horror as they beat an old man unconscious, leaving him where he fell, and kicked out at a young woman who tried, in vain, to flee from her attackers.

Even the children were not immune from the Romans' frenzy of violence. James saw one plucked from the ground effortlessly, lifted high above the soldier's head, before being launched as far as the man could throw him, to the cheers and encouragement of his fellow soldiers.

He saw the Decanus, Lucius Asina, cracking his whip in the direction of any villager that came too close, and the pleasure on his face as it connected with the flesh of his victims was obvious. Each time an ugly red welt appeared almost instantly, with blood sometimes oozing from the wounds. He fought the impulse to leave his position and offer help to those under attack; he resisted the urge to retaliate on their behalf; he was acutely aware that this was no school rugby match and to lose meant the likelihood of death. So he remained where he was, tight-lipped, and watched helplessly as the suffering continued; his contempt for Asina and the soldiers intensifying by the minute.

Then, before he knew what was happening, he felt a strong pair of hands grip his lifeless legs, and he was yanked unceremoniously from his hiding place. Trying to grab on to a stout branch, he was immediately forced to let go when a long thorn penetrated deep into the palm of his hand. Other thorns tore at his clothing and skin, drawing blood in numerous places. Although he fought with all his strength, his legs had no life in them and offered little in the way of resistance. Finally, he was free of the bush and found himself staring at the sandaled feet of his assailant.

The soldier looked down on him and smiled an evil smile sending a shiver down James' spine. He was determined not to show his fear though and instead stared at the soldier impassively. The man misconstrued his bravery as confrontational and swung a fist. James failed to see it coming. As it connected with his cheek bone, his vision began to swim even before his brain registered the sharp smarting of the blow. Catching his breath, James fought off the momentary feeling of nausea as the pain hit. Then his vision cleared and, in a moment of defiance, he looked up once more to the soldier's face, staring straight into his eyes. The soldier was incensed and struck him again and this time, James slumped backwards, unconscious. He was, for a while, free of any pain: the pain of witnessing such suffering being inflicted on the helpless people, and the pain his physical body would experience when he awoke.

Suddenly, as the soldier continued to stare, a spark of recognition crossed his face. He knew where he had seen James before and knew that Decanus Asina would reward him for his capture. Pulling a length of cord from his belt, he tied James' wrists and ankles together. Then, with apparent ease, he lifted him, slung him over his shoulder and looked around for his superior officer.

Asina was in the process of whipping a fallen man who had little to offer in the way of resistance. Each crack of the whip shredded the man's robe without touching his flesh. The man cowered, motionless, to avoid the lash, which made Asina laugh. Two more strokes and the robe fell from the man's shoulders and he clutched it as it reached his waist.

Suddenly, the soldier carrying the unconscious James appeared and it caught Asina's attention. He turned around, lowering his whip as he did so, giving the man he'd been tormenting the opportunity to scuttle off into some nearby bushes.

"What have you got there, Tobias?"

"This man, Decanus, I found him in the bushes. I recognised him from the village down the coast. I was about to kill him, but I thought that you might like the pleasure of that yourself."

"What possible interest would I have in a fisherman?"

"If you would look at his face, Decanus…"

Asina lifted James' head by his hair and stared at him.

"You have done well, soldier, and I will reward you well for this," he said. The recognition had been instant. "This one will suffer for a long time. Take him to one of the buildings and guard him – make sure he doesn't escape!"

The soldier acknowledged his commander, walking briskly away towards a building at the edge of the village.

By nightfall, the pillaging and rampaging soldiers had all but exhausted their energy and, having been banned from drinking for the night – much to their annoyance – settled into an irritable rest mode.

Slowly, James' eyes opened and he tried, unsuccessfully, to focus on the dusty floor in front of him. He was unable to move his legs and arms, either. Memories of his confrontation came to him suddenly and with them, a great hammering inside his head. Gasping involuntarily with this sudden onslaught of pain, he made no effort to move, trying instead to will some semblance of control over it. When he turned his head, his eyes watered at the pain and effort, so he decided to wait a while longer before he attempted to move again. And with that, he let himself drift back into oblivion.

When James awoke again some time later, the pain felt slightly duller and he was able to think more clearly and look around his prison. As he tested the strength of the cords tethering him, beads of sweat broke out on his forehead – they were tight and unyielding. He struggled for a futile further ten minutes before admitting that his initial escape plan would have to be amended.

Voices from outside reached his ears and the door opened.

"Looks like you've awakened right on time. You'll never guess who wants to see you or what he plans to do to you," taunted his captor.

James said nothing, pretending to roll his head and close his eyes. The soldier was having none of it and emptied half a bucket of water over his victim's head.

James gasped, but managed to swallow enough water to relieve the dryness in his mouth.

"Try not to go back to sleep. The Decanus has more fun when his victims are awake."

And with that, he drew a knife and sliced through the leather straps binding James' feet. He took a handful of James' hair and almost dragged him outside.

James heard the sound of many voices and could see the glow of a large fire ahead and guessed that they were going to the main communal area of the village. Once there, the soldier pushed him unceremoniously in front of a group of soldiers, all of whom wore the uniform of the Decanus.

Lucius Asina thanked the man and threw him a small leather purse that jangled with coins. He drew a dagger from a sheaf attached to his belt and stood up. He walked slowly and deliberately towards James, who had managed to rise unsteadily to his feet, despite the fact that his hands were still tied.

Although inwardly steeling himself for what might come next, James held a defiant stare, looking straight into Asina's eyes and, even when the knife was held up in front of his face, managed to maintain his gaze.

"You are either incredibly brave or incredibly stupid, fisherman. What do they call you?" In a show of arrogance and confidence in his own power, the Roman knelt down in front of James and severed the ties binding his hands together.

James did not react, trying instead not to reveal the pain he was experiencing as the blood flowed back to his fingers.

Strutting around his victim, Asina drew his whip, flexing its coils, before allowing the end to fall to the floor as he circled.

James kept his eyes to the front and made no effort to move.

Twice Asina circled, now appearing to measure the distance between himself and James, before lifting the whip and making it crack above his head.

James did not even flinch.

"Would you like to plead for your life, fisherman?" taunted Asina.

James remained impassive.

"It would seem that you need a little incentive to speak."

Still James said nothing.

Asina cracked the whip, as fast and lethal as a cobra's strike. This time, the tip connected with James' cheek raising a red welt, but not quite breaking the skin.

James couldn't help but flinch; the contact was a shock and the sting was powerful. He resisted the urge to check out the wound but instead remained in the same position, steadfast and impassive.

"Are you one of those who believe in this 'one god', or are you just immune to pain? Hmm? No, I saw you flinch at the touch of the lash. You feel pain all right. So tell me, does this God of yours protect only those it chooses? Because it isn't doing much of a job protecting you now, is it?"

As he finished asking the question, the whip cracked twice more and a livid welt rose on both of James' forearms.

"Still not a sound from you – no plea for mercy. What a strange man you are! Well, since you are apparently enjoying this, I won't disappoint my audience. Let's see how many places I can make you bleed."

The whip cracked time and time again, and now James could not help but clutch at each new swelling. He still resisted the urge to cry out, and was strengthened by the fact that his attacker did not seem to want to kill him, or at least not yet,

Asina soon grew bored with his task.

"As you can see, I have spared your body from too much loss of blood, fisherman. There is good reason for that, because tomorrow I will lead an attack to rid the world of those cursed with leprosy. I suspect that they will not give up easily, so I am going to provide them with some entertainment. You! I will show them what it is like to be whipped to death; a fate that will befall all those who do not comply with the wishes of the Roman Empire. Sleep well tonight, fisherman, because it will be the last night you see on this Earth."

James remained expressionless and silent. His body hurt in many places, but he used the pain to fuel his anger. He knew he wouldn't sleep tonight, however. Once the adrenaline and anger subsided, he was, no doubt, going to feel the pain all the more intensely. His thoughts were interrupted by the sound of Asina's voice again.

"Take him away and guard him well, for tonight's entertainment was but a mere taster of what is to come tomorrow."

Conflict

As predicted, the soldiers came just before noon, marching along the cliff top path. Fifty of the world's most disciplined fighting force – the Roman army. They marched with purpose and in perfect step and, from their hideout, David and Jeremiah watched as they passed by. As soon as they were out of hearing distance, Jeremiah sent David on his way down a steep, hidden path to the beach, while he jogged back towards the village the army had just left. It took David just a few minutes to descend the steep path before he was sprinting to find Arte and the rest of the community.

Arte disappeared into the cave system when the warning cry went up; David had been spotted and everybody knew that the moment they had been dreading had arrived. The men formed a line three people deep, with the women behind them. Matt, Jarrod, and Andrew took up position just in front of them and waited for Arte to rejoin them. None were prepared for the sight of him in full Roman military regalia as he emerged from the cave. Now that his robes had been dispensed with, the muscle definition of his body was on full display and, although he was a smaller man than Jeremiah, he was still an impressive sight.

"So that's what was in the bundle David fetched," Matt said to himself, noting the Arte's physique. This man would present well at any modern-day rugby match!

"I had hoped that I would never have to wear this uniform

again, in choosing a more peaceful way of life, but it appears that I am to be haunted by it," said the Tribune ruefully.

"Let us hope that it is just a temporary setback on your peaceful quest," Matt told him, not without sympathy. "What are you hoping to gain by wearing it?"

"As a senior officer, I hope to persuade the soldiers in a different direction than attacking people incapable of defending themselves. With luck I am regarded as missing rather than dead and haven't yet been branded a deserter. If so, my orders might be taken without question and bloodshed will be prevented. If the opposite is true, then I will be as much at risk as the lepers," he finished, with a sigh.

"We will outnumber the soldiers when Jeremiah brings the other village. Hopefully, when they see we're armed, even if it is only with the farmers' tools, it will be sufficient to prevent them attacking. This would only be a temporary delay, anyway, because they would simply retreat and plan a different attack, one that would place the odds squarely with them," Matt reasoned.

Arte gave the order to march and the community started moving down the beach towards the lepers' caves and, although not as disciplined or synchronised in their marching as the soldiers, they were equally determined. The plumes on Arte's helmet arched backward and his armour clanged as he led the group; an impressive soldier leading a group of men and women who conveyed an unconvincing military bearing when compared to that of the man who led them.

The march took less than a quarter an hour and soon the community was placed just beyond the lepers' cave system, tightly against the cliff face. The path leading down from the top of the cliff that the soldiers were using didn't approach the actual cliff face until the last ten metres, so the Romans would have no idea that a welcoming committee was waiting for them until it was too late.

It wasn't long before the thud of the soldiers' synchronised steps reached the community's ears and, once again Arte, Jarrod, and Matt took up position ahead of the others –

they were to be the first the soldiers would see. The footfall grew louder, beating rhythmically like a drummer marking time, until the first in line appeared before them. James was nowhere to be seen and Matt wondered what he was up to.

Arte waited for them all to reach the flat of the sand and then barked an order for the Romans to halt. They were so disciplined that they stopped to a man in perfect unison, despite the fact that it wasn't their leader who had halted them.

"Tribune Septavia! I believed you to be dead – a victim of the thieves and murderers that haunt the night in the poorer regions of this awful land," Lucius Asina called out, a mocking tone to his voice.

"As you see, I have neither fallen foul to such people, nor indeed am I dead."

"Then why is it you are hiding here with the filth of this community?" asked Lucius Asina scornfully, making no attempt to hide his disgust.

"These people are our allies. They are assisting me in rooting out spies, those who conspire against Caesar. I have been moving about as one of them, which is why I have this unkempt appearance. When I heard you were coming, I donned my uniform once more so that you would recognise me."

"Why is it that I was not privy to such information?"

"There are some within the ranks collaborating with those against Caesar, indeed, some are of significant position. The fewer people that know of my mission, the less likely the traitors will be to escape my investigations."

"This is a most convenient explanation for your disappearance, but how would I know if you are telling the truth or merely concealing the fact that you are, in fact, one of these purported collaborators?"

"You dare to challenge the word of a Tribune?"

"I dare because you are not acting in the true nature of a Tribune. One undertaking such a mission would not explain himself in front of all these men. In fact, he would not have explained himself at all, but slit my throat with his sword at my inference."

"You are observant and a true Roman. But your conduct as a soldier of the Roman army of late, begs a number of questions."

Now, it was the Decanus' turn to question what Arte had implied. "What do you mean by that? My men and I have carried out every last order we have received on behalf of our Caesar."

"Were you ordered to go around killing innocent people after you and your men had drunk so much wine as to cloud one's reason? Were you ordered you to attack the leper colony here? There is nothing to be gained by such an assault, save to satisfy your unnatural bloodlust."

The soldier standing just behind his leader started to pull out his sword. Matt saw the movement and, without thinking, ran a few short steps, quickly building momentum and launched his body in a perfect rugby tackle, taking the soldier down from just above the waist. The man stayed down, trying desperately to fill his empty lungs with air after the force of the tackle.

"Matthew, I urge you to withdraw and stand down!" thundered the Tribune.

Matt's face turned red at the rebuke but he did as ordered.

Asina placed his hand on the hilt of his sword as he kicked out at the stricken soldier and glanced at Matt with a malevolent, menacing look that threatened murder. Several other soldiers placed their hands on their weapons, but a sound from the trail announced Jeremiah's arrival, along with the community from the stricken village. The combined population of the two villages now surrounded the Roman soldiers, hemming them tightly against the cliff face, and a third group appeared at the entrances to the lepers' caves.

Men and women of all ages, covered in robes and bandages concealing their hands, feet and faces, began to move towards the soldiers. They walked down to the water's edge and approached the mass of humanity gathered along the shore line. As they drew level with them, they changed direction, walking directly and resolutely towards them. The communities split on either side of the soldiers while the lepers walked to within a few feet of them.

"Send them away from us, so they will not spread their accursed disease to the Roman Empire," bellowed Asina.

Arte moved forward, standing alongside the leading member of the leper colony, whose form was so shrouded in clothing that it was unclear if they were male or female. He nodded to Matt who stood on the other side of the leper.

"I will do no such thing! They might be afflicted with disease, but they are free people who live in peace and keep away from those without the disease. They are prepared to stand before you to protect their rights as free people, and I will stand alongside them."

"As will I," said Jeremiah, walking over to stand beside Arte.

David followed suit and stood between them and the next group of lepers and then the two communities closed in to form one united mass against the soldiers. Jeremiah smiled at David with great pride. David clutched at Jeremiah's robe and whispered something to him. The giant man turned and passed it on to Arte and then Matt, whose face took on an angry countenance.

Asina and his soldiers had their hands over their mouths and noses, desperately trying to filter the air they breathed to avoid the possibility of contamination. For the first time they looked afraid – really afraid.

"We are going to keep you here overnight, surrounded by people who should not intimidate you and yet who instil more fear than the largest of armies. By the morning, you should all be infected with the disease – that should ensure that you pay adequately for your crimes against humanity."

"That will not be happening, Tribune!" sneered Asina. "I have a prisoner who, I believe, is important to you. If you do not let us go, he will be the first to die."

A movement behind him showed a soldier leading James

to the front. Matt glared at Asina when he saw the injuries on James body.

"Are you alright, James?" Matt asked his friend.

"It looks worse than it is," replied James, speaking for the first time in almost twenty-four hours.

"He does have a voice after all! Let's see if I can make him squeal like a pig," mocked Asina, drawing his knife.

Matt didn't waste another second; the fact that Asina was by far the bigger man did nothing to deter Matt's charge, nor did the knife wielded by the Roman. Asina hadn't anticipated such an attack and, for once, was slow to react. Matt took him low in the stomach, the perfect tackle, forcing the air violently from Asina's lungs. His knife fell to the ground and before Asina could regain his footing, the impressive figure of Arte stood over him with the tip of his sword pointed at the man's throat.

Jeremiah had moved equally quickly, already untying James, having sent the young man's guard flying into his comrades with an almighty shove. No other soldier had moved, still desperately covering their mouths in an attempt to escape breathing the diseased air.

"Tribune, let us go before we are afflicted. We will leave this place and not return, on the lives of my wife and children, I swear it!" Asina showed himself in his true light, to the disgust of many of his men.

"If I let you go and hear of you committing any crime elsewhere, I will spread the word throughout the entire Roman Empire that the Decanus Lucius Asina and his army were defeated by a group of unarmed lepers. Imagine the shame and dishonour that would bring each of you. And, should that not be enough, a death sentence would certainly be issued against all those who had participated in bringing the army into disrepute.

"I will allow everyone to leave except you, Lucius. None of you will utter a word about my presence here, nor will you ever return. You will be free to question what I have questioned; to seek the truth as I have and ask yourself whether the Roman gods are false gods. Listen for the voice within, the voice of the one true God who brings peace unimaginable to the lives of his followers, and follow what His voice tells you."

With that, the crowd in front of the soldiers moved slowly aside, creating a gap sufficient for them to pass through. Matt and James restrained Lucius by the arms, preventing him from following his men.

"Drop your weapons on the beach as you leave," ordered the Tribune and he watched the soldiers relieve themselves of their weaponry."

Lucius pulled against his captors. "What are you going to do with me?" he snarled viciously at them.

"Your fate is already sealed, Lucius," answered Arte. "Take him to one of the caves, tie him up and leave two of the villagers guarding him," he continued.

The leading lepers turned and faced the Tribune and Jeremiah, bowing their heads in thanks, before slipping silently away. The two village communities mingled for a short while, sharing a new-found sense of pride, before they too began to drift back to their village or back to the boats.

James and Matt said their goodbyes to Jeremiah and Arte before heading back to their own vessel.

"What did they do to you, James?" Matt asked gently. "I hadn't even known you were in trouble."

"I was lucky, Matt, really lucky! I was stung a few times with the whip, that's all, but I could have been killed. If I didn't realise it before, then I know now for sure; we are certainly *not* invincible when we travel into the past." He sounded chastened.

"I'm glad you're ok James and that you've been through a rough ordeal, but I'm not going to shy away from what I have to say. It was selfish of you to go off without me. Look at the result! There's a strong chance this wouldn't have happened if we'd stayed together. I understand you had strong feelings but you let them outweigh common sense."

"You're right Matt, I was stupid and I'm sorry. It won't happen again. From now on we stay together."

Matt nodded satisfied. "I'll ask Martha to come and check over your injuries, just in case, if that's alright?" suggested Matt. He refrained from commenting further on his friend's revelations and apology but was clearly still mulling it over.

"That will be just fine, Matt," said James, aware that his friend needed to do something to help him.

Life in the Suburbs

Soon all the boats were full and floating once again on the water. As James looked back at the caves to wave to Arte, Jeremiah and David, another figure stood atop the cliff. James brought Matt's attention to it.

"I'm pretty sure that's Simon up there."

Matt nodded and watched as a second figure appeared and stood beside the first.

"I have no idea who that is, though."

The two figures raised their hands in a time-honoured wave of recognition.

Matt and James responded in kind, as they stood on the modest boat that bore them gently back to the village.

After the activity and excitement of the previous days, life in the village soon resumed its customary slow pace. Matt, as usual, suffered from the inactivity and spoke to James about returning home.

"I still think there is more to accomplish here," replied James. "Yes, it is different from our other adventures, in so much that we don't have such a pivotal role to play, but, you know, I've started to look at this like a rugby match."

"If this is like a rugby match then I must be pursuing the wrong sport. I've seen more action on a dartboard! It's driving me crazy."

"I can see that! I was feeling the same way until I thought about it on a different level."

"Explain…"

"Okay, rugby is a team game and the outcome of the match often depends on the performance of the team as a whole, rather than the individual. Of course, all team members want to improve their personal performance as the season progresses, and we all want to be voted man of the match – that's personal pride. But in some matches you can do a lot without really being noticed, you can play well without doing anything significant. In other matches you can have long periods of inactivity. It doesn't necessarily mean that you're playing badly; it's just one of those games that you don't seem to be able to put a personal influence on."

"I hear what you're saying. So you think that the latter is how this adventure is going?"

"Yes! Think about it for a moment. We've been here for about three weeks now, and we have impacted the game several times but have not been at the forefront of everything. Here, there are several significant members of the team who each have vital and active roles and are dominating the game more."

"Simon, Arte, Jeremiah, David as well as us?"

"Don't forget the Rabbi. We may not have met him yet, but he seems to have a significant role, especially in his affect on Simon, Jeremiah and Arte."

"You're right, and I accept the points you've made, but, to be honest, it doesn't really change how I feel right now. If you're correct about everything, how will we ever know when our work is done and the adventure is over?"

"We will know, Matt. We *always* know and I don't think it'll be any different here."

"Let's go for a run and do some training then. It is what we'd originally planned to do this summer."

"I'd welcome the distraction as much as you, but the problem is that we're dressed in robes and I've never seen anybody here dressed otherwise for any purpose."

"Power-walking along the beach in the sand, then – we can do that, surely?"

"That sounds better than staying here in leafy suburbia!" joked James.

They managed to work up a good sweat on their walk and when they were several miles from the community, removed their robes so they could swim unencumbered in the surf. Afterwards, lying on the sand to dry off in the sun, James spotted a small boat with a single figure on it. As it approached, Jeremiah's familiar features were instantly recognisable. The boys quickly slipped their robes back on, standing to wave. Almost instantly, the boat changed course and headed for them, with Jeremiah waving back. As the boat came to a stop in the sand, Jeremiah grinned a boyish grin that belied his real age.

"Shalom, my friends! It is good to see you again!"

"Shalom, Jeremiah!" responded Matt and James, in perfect harmony.

"You've finished the boat! I can't believe that you've finished it so quickly!"

"I have been working all hours on it, with the help of Arte and David. Today is the boat's maiden voyage, so I thought I would come and visit my good friends."

"And show off the boat?"

"It has been a long time since I have used my carpentry skills and it has pleasured me in its making," Jeremiah answered, a little bashfully.

"It's a fine boat, Jeremiah! How does it handle?" asked James.

"It is very responsive and I think this is because of the deeper keel I've given it. It has a much smoother ride."

"How would you feel about showing it off to us, on the water, back to the village?"

"It would be my pleasure, come aboard!"

It didn't take them long to return to the village. Jeremiah was absolutely correct about how the boat handled, and how much more stable the ride felt.

"I think the other fishermen will want to experience this for themselves. If all goes well, Jeremiah, you might get some business from this."

"That is an idea I had not thought of. My true purpose in coming back was to find some more nets, so that I might fish for Arte and the lepers. He believes that he can make a difference to their quality of life and wants to take every opportunity to do just that."

"What about you Jeremiah? Will you stay at the caves or come back to the village?"

"I am not yet sure. My path has not been shown to me. I was hoping that Simon would be able to make some suggestions, or perhaps take me to see the Rabbi who always seems to have something positive to suggest."

"We haven't met the Rabbi yet. What's he like?"

"A true holy man – a man who is at peace with himself and what he believes; a man who sees the good in the world before the bad and who helps those who are suffering or in need."

"Perhaps we could meet him sometime?" suggested Matt.

"It is Simon who arranges most of the meetings with him. He is trying to lead the type of life that the Rabbi instructs, and it is clear that the Rabbi favours him."

As the boats keel dug into the sand, a crowd started to gather. Jeremiah received a welcome far greater than he would have done a few weeks ago. It was clear that the man was changing, moving toward something. The question was – what? His new boat caused a few raised eyebrows and, for the next hour, he gave rides to the curious fishermen so they could experience the differences in the boat's feel and design first-hand. Needless to say, they were all highly impressed.

Andrew suggested an informal gathering to celebrate Jeremiah's accomplishments and invited him to share a meal with him that evening. As always, Martha invited Matt and James, her gratitude to Matt for saving Jarrod's life was ever-present. If she had something to offer him, she gave with an open heart. Besides, she also wanted to apply some more of her healing salve to James' wounds, although he felt there was little need for this.

After the meal, as darkness fell, the community gathered at the communal building and good-natured banter became the natural order of the evening. Halfway through the evening, Jeremiah asked the fishermen for some old nets and explained the reason he wanted them. Immediately, two nets were promised to him, but he was told that they were not in the best of conditions.

An older fisherman, Benjamin, offered to make him a new net as he no longer joined his sons on their boat and, in return, Jeremiah promised to make his sons a new boat. Benjamin was quick to point out that the exchange was hardly fair, so Jeremiah suggested that the new boat should replace the old one, which he could then sail away and make modifications to.

"A new net and an old boat is a very good price for a new boat! Are you sure that you are satisfied with your end of the bargain, Jeremiah?" the old man asked.

"I am more than happy, Benjamin. With two boats in my fleet, I can fish for the great shoals as this community does."

"Then we have a deal, my friend, and I will start on the new net tomorrow."

He was as good as his word for, shortly after dawn, Matt and James passed him on the beach, working away with some sinuous twine that would eventually become Jeremiah's new net.

As the two continued their walk, they noticed a waving figure on the cliff top above them and recognised Simon. They returned the wave and changed direction to intercept him on the path that descended to the beach.

"Shalom, my friends! How have you been?"

"We are well, Simon. And you?"

The three fell into casual conversation as they walked towards the village. Matt told Simon about Jeremiah, the boat and the deal he had struck with Benjamin, and he looked highly pleased. Then Simon talked about their part in supporting the lepers on the beach, against the Roman soldiers, and how pleased he was that it all ended peacefully, without further bloodshed.

They sat down together before they reached the village and discussed the change in Jeremiah and how happy he now seemed, though Matt mentioned that the man felt he had not yet found his calling in the way that Arte had.

"Every man has a role to play, Matthew. You and James have been playing your own important part for a while now and, although you may not feel that way, it is true nevertheless."

James eyed Simon with curiosity.

"How is it that you know how Matt and I are feeling, Simon?"

"The Rabbi has given me some understanding of the ways of men, and what he says is true. All men need to feel that they contribute to something, that they are part of something that makes their lives seem purposeful. You have just begun to seek your own paths, through actions more than words, and I tell you now that your lives will soon change, in a big way, when you have finished the work that has been set for you."

"We don't even know what that work is," said Matt sadly, and with more than a little confusion.

"Sometimes, it feels as if you don't know, as if you are stumbling in the dark and then all of a sudden, you're involved in something so deeply significant to the lives of others, such as what you did for the leper community."

"How long will all this take, Simon?" James asked.

"What you are doing is God's work. You cannot put a time limit on it, for it is merely the blink of an eye for Him, whereas it may be half a lifetime for us. There is one who He would have you help find his own path. You already know this man and that is your next task, of this I am sure. Now, let us go to the village for I am hungry and thirsty, and wish to see those I have not seen for some time."

Matt and James walked in silence, thinking deeply about what Simon had. When they reached the village and Simon started to greet those who came to meet him, they walked on to their house and prepared a light meal of their own.

"What do you make of what he said, James?"

"Well, he sort of told us that our work here is not quite finished, but will be soon. There is somebody who needs our help still, and this is probably our final task. How on earth does he know all this?"

"I've no idea! I wonder who he's talking about?" Matt refused to be side-tracked by his friend.

"I would hazard a guess at it being Jeremiah."

"What makes you so sure?"

"Think about it! Arte is already on his path, Jeremiah told us that. David is happy enough in helping both Jeremiah and Arte – it's almost like he has two fathers looking out for him, and he deserves that. He's a good boy. And Simon? Well, Simon seems to be the most sorted guy I've ever met, which just leaves Jeremiah. Although we've had dealings with other people here, none of them have been as significant as Jeremiah. And didn't Jeremiah himself tell us about wanting to visit the Rabbi to find his calling in life?"

Directions

The next morning, a strengthening wind was blowing from the east that deterred all the fishermen from venturing to sea.

Matt and James had decided to put their heads together, to see if they could perhaps come up with a vocation for Jeremiah. They rejected all their initial ideas, so James suggested a walk away from the beach and the village to clear their thoughts and perhaps help generate some inspiration. They elected to go up the cliff path and up into the hills, to follow some of the route that had led them to the village when they had first arrived.

Matt, of course, led the way, setting a hard pace while telling James that the climb would be good for their leg muscles, but James knew that his friend was still feeling frustrated at the lack of action. Coming to a small stream that suggested they had gone off of course, as they hadn't passed it originally, they stopped to refresh themselves and quench their thirst. Then, they lay back on the grassy bank.

"Does this remind you of the day we first found the cave leading to the time portal, James?"

"You mean the day that we decided to use swimming as part of our fitness training, only to discover that we weren't particularly good at it?"

Matt laughed. "Trust you to think of the negative! A

few more days of practice and we'd have started to feel the benefit."

Suddenly, there was a rustling sound to their left, in some low-lying scrub bushes.

"Did you hear that?"

"I heard something," Matt replied, sitting up and staring at the area the sound had come from.

"Probably a goat or something. Come on, let's go on a bit further. It's good to get away from the sand for a change."

"That's true, the stuff gets everywhere! Even the food is gritty, at times."

They crossed a meadow of thigh-length grass with tall, wispy plants bearing violet flowers. The hills beyond the meadow were sparser, in terms of vegetation, with large clumps of rocks dividing the scenery into smaller, defined sections. The boys continued to trudge slowly upward, with no real purpose other than to enjoy the time alone and the exercise the walk was giving them.

They had been walking a good while when James spotted movement amongst some rocks up ahead and peered to try to see what it was.

"It looks like there are more goats up ahead, hidden behind the rocks. I wonder if they belong to somebody, or if they are a wild herd." James voiced his thoughts aloud.

"Let's head over to where you saw them and rest before heading back. It's well after noon now, and we want to be off these slopes before it gets dark."

"Sounds good to me! I hope Martha's been cooking for us again, because we're going to be very hungry when we get back."

"Do you think we're taking advantage of her? We've hardly had to cook for ourselves at all, since saving Jarrod."

"That was a good day's work for more than one reason then, Matt!" James joked.

It was Matt who next noticed movement among the rocks.

"You're right, there's definitely something up ahead. I couldn't make out whether it was goats or not, though."

When they reached the rock pile a few minutes later, there were no animals to be seen, so they sat and rested, looking around to see if the goats might reappear.

Passing the water carrier between them they both drank enthusiastically, despite the water being rather warm. James laid it down at his side and held his face to the warm breeze. He closed his eyes and enjoyed its gentle caress on his face. Neither spoke for a few minutes, as they both sat enjoying the peace of the desolate place.

After a while James stretched, announcing that it was time to go and reached down for the water carrier which, to his surprise, was no longer where he had put it.

"Have you got the water carrier, Matt?" he asked.

"No, I gave it back to you."

James searched around the rocks surrounding the place where they were sitting.

"That's weird! I *know* I put it by my side and now it's disappeared."

"It can't have done – unless a goat took it! You did say you thought you saw goats."

"I did, but now I'm thinking that it wasn't goats at all, but something else. I've a feeling we've got company, Matt.

Looking around briefly, James whispered, "Humour me. Walk up the path until you pass the next pile of rocks, then climb over them to double back. I'm going to do the same thing down the path. If there's somebody here, we'll certainly be able to see them from higher up."

They separated, doing what James had suggested.

All of a sudden, Matt disappeared between two very large boulders and gave a shout of triumph.

James hopped nimbly from rock to rock until he reached his friend. Squealing, followed by curses from Matt betrayed the fact that he was no longer alone.

"What have you found, Matt?"

"You were right! It wasn't a goat – it's a young girl, I think, although from the state of her, I can't be too sure. She has our water-carrier too, which makes her a little thief!"

He lifted her up out of the rocks, so James could see for himself. James took hold of her, allowing Matt the opportunity to climb out, but almost lost his grip as she bit down hard on his hand, drawing blood. Between them, they carried the wriggling, squealing child out of the rocks and onto a section of grass, where they took a firm grip of a hand each, forcing her to sit down.

"What's your name, girl?" asked Matt

She made no attempt to answer but tried to bite his hand instead. The boys tightened their grip on her and asked her again. Still, she refused to reply although she did cease her struggling somewhat. Then a stone hit James squarely on the thigh.

"Ouch! What the heck was that?" he asked. But before he could get an answer, another hit him in the chest with sufficient force to make him release the girl's wrist.

Matt received three blows in quick succession, two on the legs and one to the upper arm. He, too, involuntarily let go of the girl's hand as he instinctively rubbed the places of impact. The girl immediately jumped up and ran back towards the rocks and, as James and Matt stood to give chase, a flurry of stones came flying towards them.

"Forget the girl! Let's get out of here before we get hit in the head," shouted Matt, speeding off down the path with James hard at his heels.

They stopped fifty or so metres from their original position and looked back. There, on the rock pile, was a group of about ten children, still launching missiles towards them. By the state of their robes, they were clearly homeless.

"The little monsters! It's no wonder Jeremiah used to get so cross with them, if that's the way they carry on," said Matt, rubbing his bruised arm as they started back towards the village.

"Got to hand it to them though, Matt said suddenly laughing, it was a very good team performance back there!"

"Yes, but for what? A water carrier! It's hardly worth all that effort, is it?"

"I suppose such things are beyond their means, or it gives them something to sell, if nothing else. Think how hard it must be for these kids, if even the communities are finding life hard."

"They need help. You'd think they'd be put in an orphanage or something."

"But they probably don't even exist, yet."

"Yes, but it's obviously what they need!" They continued in silence for a couple of minutes, before the boys suddenly paused, almost as one, and looked at each other.

James spoke first, "Hang on a minute, Matt. I think I may have an idea."

"I'm on the same page already, if you're thinking of a certain bearded giant who currently resides in a massive cave system…"

"The same man that builds boats and wants to fish for the people of the leper colony?"

"I have a feeling that Jeremiah might like this idea. He could go from being a single man, to having a huge family overnight!"

"There could be a problem gathering all the homeless children around here, and even then, they might not want to go and stay with him."

"I think that David could well have a part to play in that. The kids have a lot to gain by going to live with Jeremiah; they could learn really useful skills such as boat-building, fishing and farming, which might help them in later life. And they'd have regular meals and proper beds at night. They'd be looked after by a decent and caring man who could also teach them about right from wrong."

"You're right – this is a great idea and everybody wins! I can't wait to get back to tell him."

The children, still throwing the occasional missiles in their direction, were soon left behind as Matt and James walked briskly back to the village. Arriving just as the sun started to dip below the horizon, they looked eagerly around for Jeremiah.

Martha noticed them arrive and asked them who they were looking for. She told them that Jeremiah had left the village earlier, with Simon, to go and speak with the Rabbi.

"Foiled again!" exclaimed Matt. "You know, we really ought to go and meet this Rabbi, James. He's such an influential figure around here; I want to see what all the fuss is about."

"I know what you mean, but I'm sure that our paths will cross soon."

"It rather spoils the evening plans, though, with Jeremiah being away. I was really looking forward to telling him our idea."

"Me too, but it can wait until tomorrow."

Martha smiled fondly at them and invited them to eat with her and Jarrod again that evening. They accepted happily, with a small sidelong glance at each other, but looked forward to running their ideas by her and her husband as they ate.

Later that evening, it appeared that both their hosts liked the new idea, anticipating that Jeremiah would too, but were also concerned about how hard it would be to persuade the children to try living under his guidance.

"They don't trust anybody," said Martha, with more than a little sadness in her voice.

"We're hoping that David will be useful there, after all, he was one of them once, and he too found it difficult to trust anybody. Ultimately, he was just waiting for the right opportunity to come along."

"It is a good idea but, even so, I do not think it will be enough," continued Martha.

"Perhaps we might have to do something rather more radical, then," said Matt.

"What do you mean?"

"What if we were just to round them up and take them to the caves by boat? We could let them see what's on offer, fill their bellies and then leave them there, letting them choose whether to stay with Jeremiah and Arte, or to walk back to the hills when we've gone."

"This is not a good way to go about it, Matthew," said

Martha. "It will not help inspire trust in these unfortunate children."

"It has to be better than being taken by the soldiers to be sold as slaves, which is their likely fate the longer they're separated from adults who can help them. They just need to know that they can come and go as they please, only after they've seen what it could be like, if they would just give it a try."

"What you are saying is right, but your method to achieve it is not. If I were you, I would ask Simon to speak with them. He is a gentle man that the children all respect. He has also been kinder to them than most others, and has a way of speaking that inspires people. This is what I think you should do."

"Simon is not the only one who has a way with words, Martha. Thank you for sharing your thoughts with us. I will speak with him when he returns."

Challenge

It was early the next day when Matt and James set out to see Simon. Since he regularly left the village on the Rabbi's business, they were unsure whether they would find him at home. But, the gentle man opened his door to them at the first knock and invited them inside.

"How can I help you, my friends?"

"We have been thinking about what you told us, about finding our purpose here and how it was concerned with helping others," Matt started.

"We think that the person or persons we need to help, is Jeremiah and the homeless children," continued James.

"How was it that you came to this conclusion?" asked Simon, giving no hint at all of whether their thoughts were accurate or not.

Carefully, James explained, mentioning the people who had been most prominent in their lives, since they had returned to the village, and the involvement that the two of them had had with each.

"The good things that people do are often overshadowed by the greater needs of existence: finding food, paying taxes and avoiding conflict with the Romans, for example. The two of you have had quite an impact on those around you with the good that you do. The people now think of you, Matthew, as one of their own, where once you were seen as an enemy," said Simon. "The thoughts you have are good and, yet again, you seek to help others with no thought of personal gain. It is what He expects of his people and, I think, you have earned a special place in His heart already.

"Take your ideas and work with them; put them into action and see what transpires. There is little to lose and so much to gain for the children and for the heart of our friend, Jeremiah. But, consider the possibility of involving one other; a man who is also intent on changing his life and partaking in the Lord's work. I do not need to say more, for you already know this man, but his future, as well as that of Jeremiah, may be linked to an even greater purpose, giving something of real value and meaning to those who have nothing."

"There might be a way for you to help us with one concern we have," said James, in a hopeful voice.

"I will help wherever I can, and you have only to ask. But I must advise that for the next few days, I have other duties to attend to with the Rabbi that will keep me away from here. But tell me, what is it I can do for you?"

"We wondered if you would speak to the children for us. They know you and trust you, and we can't say the same about their opinion of us."

"I think you are being too harsh upon yourselves, but if you have had no luck in convincing them, then, of course, I will speak to them on my return."

"Thank you, Simon. There is one more thing I would like to know; in truth it has been on my mind for some time. When we had all that trouble at the caves, Arte told Lucius Asina that his fate had been sealed. What did he mean by that and what happened to Asina?" asked James.

"You have no need to worry, James. Asina has not been harmed – far from it. Arte was confident that Asina, like him, could change if he had the desire and the right guidance."

"Why would a man like him want to change?" interrupted Matt.

"Everyone can change if there is incentive enough."

"But he craved only power and wealth."

"That's because he wasn't aware of any alternative. Arte took Asina to see the Rabbi, who talked to him as he has many others. Asina was so moved that he decided to stay to hear more. He is there still, learning and growing, and something tells me that when he leaves, he will be a different person."

"It would take something special to change Lucius Asina's ways," suggested Matt.

"Something or some*one*!" responded Simon who smiled warmly at them and said that it was time for him to leave. Wishing them luck, he also suggested that they pay another visit to Jeremiah and Arte.

The easterly winds had halted any chance of fishing over the past two days, and the fishermen wouldn't take to the boats until the seas calmed again. So the boys decided to walk to the caves and spend the night with their friends, before returning the following morning. Reaching the caves in the late afternoon, they were greeted warmly by Jeremiah who had noticed their approach and walked along the beach to meet them.

"Shalom, my good friends, Shalom!" he called, grinning from ear to ear.

"Shalom, Jeremiah!"

"I did not expect to see you again so soon. Tell me what brings you this way. There is no more trouble, I hope?"

"We have a proposition to discuss with you, but that must wait until we have quenched our thirst, for we have been walking a long time."

"Of course, come to the cave and I will fetch you some cooling water! Arte and David are there working on the boat I promised the village. I have already been given the old nets that I wished for and wanted to get the boat finished quickly. I would be pleased to show it to you as I have altered the keel again, in an attempt to improve the stability further; I've also made changes to the shape of the bow to make it cut through the water better and travel at a faster speed."

His excitement about the boat overshadowed his

thoughts of refreshment as he stopped at the site where it was being built. David and Arte weren't there as Jeremiah had said, which didn't seem to bother him in the slightest as he showed them around the constructed frame of the boat.

"I have plans to include a removable shelter on board where the crew can take refuge from the sun or rain. What do you think?" he finished triumphantly.

"I can see that you have everything under control and I must say that the modifications look good. I am amazed at how quickly you have achieved all of this."

Jeremiah glowed at the comments.

"Arte and David work as hard as I do, and our progress is the better for our joint efforts. Now, how about that water?"

They sat at the cave entrance, watching the white horses on the sea skip and dance their graceful performance, as Matt shared news from the village.

"Sometimes I miss community life," responded Jeremiah. "And then, sometimes I do not! Life is peaceful here and there is no need for rules and routines. It depends on the mood I am in, which is mostly good these days."

"Did you ever think about starting your own community?" asked James.

"What do you mean?"

Before he could answer, a shout from along the beach announced the arrival of Arte and David. The two were carrying lengths of wood that had already been cut and shaped where the tree had been felled.

Dropping their load by the frame of the boat, the pair hastened over to greet Matt and James. Jeremiah poured each of them a vessel of water, which was drained in an instant, before they sat requesting the news that Matt and James had already imparted to Jeremiah.

"You will join us for our evening meal?" David asked them.

"We'd be delighted to! What's on the menu?" Matt asked.

"Arte felled a wild goat with his spear, this morning, so we have meat instead of fish for a change," David told him, excitedly.

The chance to discuss their ideas disappeared as spirited preparations for the meal ensued, Jeremiah taking on the cooking duties.

Arte and James walked down to the boat where he tried positioning the last pieces of wood that he and David had cut.

"They need the skill of a master boat builder, really. David and I are getting good at selecting, cutting down, and roughly shaping wood, but only Jeremiah has the skills to shape them into the final parts ready to fit. It is time-consuming work for him with a need for precision, but once he has finished shaping, David and I can fit it. We manage to keep the process busy all the time, which is why we are able to build so quickly."

"Matthew and I have come here with a proposition for Jeremiah, but after seeing how the three of you are working so well together, I think what we have in mind may be something for you to consider as well. We will discuss it after our meal."

"It sounds intriguing, James, I am interested already!"

"Wait until you hear it first!" came the reply.

Matt had walked down to the water's edge, and was watching the curl of the wave form the tube that modern-day surfers liked to travel through.

"So how has it been here for you, David, with a new life, a fresh start and some real purpose?"

"It is good, Matthew. I have responsibilities now. I work and I get fed, that is a good feeling! Arte and Jeremiah are like fathers to me. They treat me well and care for me, I could not wish for more."

"I am glad for you, my friend. What about the family you left behind – those that still live the life you have moved away from? Do you not think that they too might like such an opportunity, the chance of a new life as you have?"

"Some of them would, of this I am sure. But there are others who have been without homes for too long and they would find the change difficult."

"Would they find it so difficult, knowing that they would have regular food, without having to beg or steal?"

"They would be most grateful for it, as I am, but the trust that involves would take a long time to build. Would they have to work for it too, like me?"

"I think there are many types of work that could be done to benefit everybody. If the children would agree to work in exchange for food and shelter, then the move to build trust is already started."

"Why do you ask me about this, Matthew?"

"Well, James and I have an idea which could benefit a lot of people, but everything depends on trust and mutual cooperation. We planned to talk about this tonight, after the meal, but there are a few things that we need to clarify with each of you first."

"I will be interested to hear more from you later then, Matthew, but that smell suggests that our meal is nearly ready."

The meal was eaten in a genial silence, and both Matt and James remembered the taste of the meat as being the same that they had eaten when they first came to the community.

"I never thought I could enjoy goat meat so much," said Matt, throwing a compliment to Jeremiah.

"I think it always tastes better mixed with some vegetables and herbs. Fortunately, the garrison cook could do amazing things with meat of all sorts, when Arte was a soldier and he happily passed on some of those ideas to me when I commented on the quality of the food he served."

"Do you miss the life of a soldier, Arte?" asked Matt.

"Not at all. Too much bloodshed and killing for dubious and even unjust reasons can take away a man's true essence. I know now that my calling is to serve God, and I am glad that I can be the opposite of what I once was."

"It is time you told me why you came to visit me, James," said Jeremiah, intrigue evident in his voice.

"We have an idea that we really hope you will like and would be prepared to take on. We think it would be everything you want in terms of giving your life purpose, meaning and direction."

"I thought I already had a new direction, a new path to follow."

"You have and this is merely an extension of it."

"So, put me out of my misery, then. What is it?

James explained their ideas, adding that the task could be extended to include Arte as well.

"The opportunity to build a new community is enormous and challenging. I can see the reasoning behind it and the good it could bring, but the responsibility of so many, especially some so young, is a daunting prospect. I will need to think on this carefully and I would also want to speak to Arte for his frank opinion and possible involvement."

"If you like, we can leave you to think it over and return next week?"

"That will not be necessary, for you could both be our guests for a few days. While the wind blows, there will be no fishing. What do you think?"

Matt and James accepted the invitation with pleasure, before leaving the cave and going for a walk along the moonlit beach with the boy David following.

Orphanage

It was almost a day before Jeremiah approached James to tell him that he had serious concerns about the idea.

"In principle, I think it is a good idea, James. But the needs of the children are many and I am not sure I could meet them all."

"Tell me your concerns, Jeremiah."

"Firstly, there is the question of food. There are times when it will be impossible to fish and sometimes harvesting what we grow will not be enough to last for the whole winter. The children would go hungry."

"What is the difference between that scenario and the one they face already on a daily basis? I cannot begin to imagine how hard it must be for those children not to know when or where their next meal is coming from."

"It is true what you say, James. But if they fall under my care, then it would be my responsibility and the thought of that would weigh heavily."

"There is more?"

"The children would need educating and, when I think of what I am good at, which is building boats and fishing, then there is little else that I can teach them."

"On this topic you are wrong, my friend. You have experience and knowledge of life; you know the difference between right and wrong and you know how to survive. These are the things they need to learn about, as well as fishing, building boats and growing food. If you ask me, I would say that these children are already ahead of the game because they know how to survive."

"It is true, perhaps I didn't look at this from the right perspective, but there is one more thing that I cannot give them."

"Which is?" James persisted, noticing that Jeremiah seemed hesitant to speak his mind.

"The children need a woman's touch, the nurturing, the loving and the gentleness. These are skills that I am not graced with."

"Jeremiah, I swear that sometimes you cannot see what is right in front of your own eyes! For some time now you have been taking care of young David. You feed him, you care for him, you laid a blanket over him last night against the chill of the wind and I have seen you play with him. If these are not signs of love, then I do not know what is. You are trying to lead your life in a different way, become a better person. What more could a child wish for in a caregiver? Already there is a vast difference in the way you are, from the man I first met. Do you not realise this?"

"I do, James, and this is partly the reason I am being so cautious. I do not want to let God down."

"I would have thought God would be more let down if you didn't try."

"It is such a huge responsibility, James. What if I tried and failed?"

"If you don't try, then you have failed already!"

James knew that he was gradually getting his point across and Jeremiah was warming to the idea. He played his final card.

"What does Arte think of all this? I am guessing that you two talked this through."

"Arte is in favour of the idea. Indeed, the caves are perfect for such a development. He has offered to help, but he is also committed to the lepers and will not rescind his promise to feed them."

"I don't see that as a problem, because you just need to catch more fish and grow more food. And that process is already underway."

"There would be a lot of work to do before the caves would be ready to live in."

"What do you need?"

"Some of the caves have very large openings and have very high roofs which make them cold and damp. They need to be walled up, preferably with clay bricks to keep away the drafts. Inside the caves, spaces need to be made for small groups of people; having too many in one place can create problems. Each area needs a hearth for a small fire to keep it warm and give light at night time and, of course, to cook food. Then there is a question of bedding; I do not have time to make so many beds from wood, so hay and straw need to be collected. It is not much to give them."

"It would be more than anybody has given them before and so much more than they have right now. All we need is a plan of action to set everything in motion, and I know just where to get the manpower we need to get the construction underway," he grinned.

Matt and James travelled back to their village the following day and spread the news of what Jeremiah and Arte were planning to do. The wind was still too strong for fishing, so James asked Andrew to call a meeting so that he could ask everyone for their help at the caves.

"To start with, we need people to help make the clay bricks and gather straw and hay. Later we'll need help to build the walls with the bricks we've made."

"I have never heard of another venture quite like this one, James, but it is a most wonderful thing. I, for one, would be pleased to offer my services until the wind breaks, for then I must go fishing. But I am happy to help with the construction of the walls when needed," volunteered Andrew.

"Martha and I will help too." Jarrod spoke next, before a chorus of people also pledged their help.

"We will walk to the caves tomorrow morning, and commence work until there is a break in the wind," said Andrew.

With this, the meeting came to an end and the community dispersed, returning to their own hearths.

"It all seems to be coming together, James," said Matt with a satisfied smile.

"Do you realise that this could well be the start of the world's first orphanage? How cool is that?"

"It means our adventure here is coming to an end, then."

"Yes, it looks that way, but I think I'd like to stay until the children move in, before we go back through the waterfall."

The community walked the distance to the caves with an excited air of anticipation. Arte and Jeremiah saw them coming from some way off and walked to meet them.

After many smiles and shaloms Jeremiah asked, "What are you all doing here?"

"We heard from Matthew and James that you want to make a home here for all the homeless children. It is a wonderful idea and we would like to help you," Andrew told him.

"I cannot believe that you all have come!" said Arte in surprise.

"Nobody has stayed behind. Perhaps you could tell us what you would like us to do, so that our time here does not go to waste."

"I will take care of that, but after we have shared a little food and water first. You have travelled a long way!"

"Food is already prepared and just needs heating. We have brought you a gift from the village," Martha handed Jeremiah a length of rope, behind which four goats were attached.

"You now have the start of your own goat herd – fresh milk every day!"

Jeremiah blinked rapidly a few times and cleared his throat. "You have been so kind and thoughtful," he said, with a catch in his voice.

After the meal, Arte deployed some of the women to

the grasslands above the cliffs to cut and collect dried grass. Others collected water to take to an area where the ground was heavy with clay. It was their job to mix water into the fairly hard clay to make it more malleable and turn it into bricks. The bricks were to be left in the sun to dry and harden; a process that could take a week or more, except that Matt suggested that they dry some around a fire built specially for the purpose. Some men were also sent to cut down trees to be used for the framework needed and for future boat-building.

By the end of the afternoon, more than enough straw and hay had been collected for the beds, but the surplus would be used by the guests for their overnight stay.

Matt's idea of drying the bricks out by the fire proved successful, as the first bricks dried quickly in this manner, and were almost ready for assembly. They were carried inside the cave to where they would be used to form a partition. Several more fires were lit that day and bricks laid around them. With the bedding sorted, more people were assigned to the brick-making, with the woodcutting team being the only exemptions from the task.

Hundreds of bricks were made that day and left to dry, and Jeremiah estimated that they had about half of what they needed. Another day like today and most of the physical work would be over, minus the actual construction. He secretly hoped that the wind would continue to blow strong for one more day.

Jeremiah's wish was granted, as the winds did not begin to let up until the following night. The men were alerted in the small hours of the morning and made their way back to the village while it was still dark. The women stayed at the caves, offering their help in another day of brick-making before they too departed, in time to help their menfolk when they returned from sea.

Jeremiah launched his own boat to go fishing too. As is often the case after the wind has blown hard for several days, he easily found a shoal of fish not long into his trip and came back with fully laden nets.

Lighting fires just inside the caves beside the accumulated stacks of bricks would speed up the drying process if kept alight for the next week or so, and Arte organised stacks of wood for this purpose. Matt and James did a fair share of the cutting and chopping as they had stayed on at the caves with them for a few extra days before returning to the village ready for their next task. This time David journeyed back with them, too.

Persuasion

The boys were in luck when they got back to the village, because Simon had already returned. They did not waste any time in going to find him.

"Shalom, Simon!"

"Shalom, my friends! I heard that you have been fruitful in the challenge we discussed. How is it you knew that Jeremiah was the one whom you needed to help?"

"It was a simple process of elimination really. We removed the less obvious choices and considered the merits of the more likely individuals."

"Your plan was excellent, and you succeeded in getting the whole village to help. I am most impressed!"

"Well, the people here are very community-minded, which is no doubt down to you, Simon."

Simon looked off into the distance, while he considered this for a moment, before answering. "The Rabbi should take more credit than I, for when he speaks, everybody listens. He has a way of bestowing peace in the hearts and minds of everyone who hears him."

"You have the same gift, Simon."

He smiled at them. "If that is true, then it is God-given, for I was not always as I am now."

"Listen, Simon do you remember me asking for your help? The caves are almost ready for their new inhabitants, but

Matthew and I think that the real difficulty is going to be convincing the children they should go."

"I can see why they might not trust people readily, especially those offering something for nothing as they will be suspicious of their motives. But that just means you will have to be more persuasive."

"We were really hoping that you would come with us and help win them over; they are more likely to trust you than anybody else."

"I would be happy to help with this, but gathering the children together will be hard. If they see a group of people heading towards them, they are more likely to scatter than risk the chance of being caught."

"Perhaps David might the key to that problem. He came back to help us with this."

"Maybe Arte and Jeremiah can help too. I suspect they are on their way to us already,"

"How could you possibly know that?" asked Matt with a grin.

"The wind is freshening again and I believe the community here made a promise to help when the wind prevents fishing."

He was absolutely right. Jeremiah and Arte appeared later that afternoon and were welcomed warmly into the village. Both men spent time with Simon before greeting Matt and James properly.

"Shalom Matthew! Shalom James!" Jeremiah gave each of them a huge bear hug that threatened to squeeze every last gasp of air from their lungs.

"How is it at the caves, Jeremiah?" asked James, rubbing his ribs ruefully.

"Arte and I have finished the first dividing wall in the main cave, but our progress is painfully slow as neither of us has skills of this nature. We are hoping that while the wind strengthens, others will come back with us to help once again."

"I don't think there will be much doubt about that. Most of them are looking forward to finishing that little project.

We need one of you to stay behind, though, to help with the children. They have little reason to trust any of us, but they do know you and David. He, especially, is going to be very important in persuading them to consider this move."

"I will stay with you. Arte is better at laying bricks than I, and he is good at overseeing what goes on, a testament to his days as Tribune, I think. Perhaps it would be a good idea for you to journey back with Arte, James. You are good with ideas and we must start thinking about turning the individual spaces into homes. Matthew, David and I can take on the challenge of the children."

James nodded, pleased that he had been thought of as an ideas man, always ready for a challenge.

"Good, now that we have everything arranged, perhaps you two would care to join Matthew and me for the evening meal."

"I would be happy to accept for both of us."

David had been spoilt by Martha since his return to the village. She had developed something of a soft spot for the boy after noticing the way he always looked after Arte and Jeremiah's needs. She had already fed him, so he wasn't hungry when he eventually made his way back to Matt and James' house.

"We have been talking about you, David. Were your ears burning?" Matt asked him, ruffling the top of his curly head affectionately.

"Since I am not on fire, do you not think that that is a strange question to ask me?"

"It's an old saying – never mind." Matt corrected himself quickly, hoping that he wouldn't have to explain further.

"What were you saying about me?"

"Only that we think your next task is very important, so important, in fact, that it might be too big for you to manage." Matt teased.

"I can manage most tasks that are set for me. What have you in mind?" he asked indignantly.

"We need you to go up into the high meadows and speak

to the homeless children. Encourage them to meet with Jeremiah, Simon and me."

"Why does this invitation not include Arte?"

"Arte is returning to the caves with James and the villagers to help build the walls. We want to finish them before the new arrivals. We plan to talk to the children, encourage them to come to the caves and help them understand that they won't be prisoners, that they'll be free to come and go as they please. They also need to appreciate that they'll all have to contribute to the community, to earn their keep. It won't be hard labour – just some chores to help with all the things that will need to be done, such as collecting firewood or water, gathering food, helping with the boats, things like that. Some of them may not wish to go now, but that's okay. If they choose to wait until things get too hard for them, like in wintertime when food is scarce, they will be welcomed then. The caves will always be a safe haven for them."

"I shall talk to them first, because they will hide before you ever got close to them! It might take a while for them to agree to meet you, but as they already know Simon and Jeremiah that should help a little. I'll go tomorrow."

"Some of them have already encountered us as well, threw a few stones at us."

"How did you react to this?"

"We let them be."

"That is good, for if you had acted otherwise they would never trust you."

The next morning David left early. He was pleased to be able to offer some of his friends the hope of something better, but he was under no illusions about the opposition and suspicion he would face. Many of the older children had had less than positive encounters with people from the village. Climbing higher and higher up the hillside, he came to the place where the youngsters had pelted James and Matt with stones, and sat down in practically the same spot to wait for them to appear. He knew that some of them were probably nearby already. It was almost fifteen minutes later that the first child decided to come out from his hiding place. He was about a year younger than him, but had been with the group for a few years and David knew him well.

"Shalom, Joshua! It has been a long while since I have seen you. How are you?"

"I am well, but pickings have been slim lately. There has not been much fishing and people are already guarding their food closely."

"Is that so? I know of a place where you can eat regularly in exchange for a little work. You can get a soft bed and shelter for as long as you want it."

Joshua eyed David sceptically. "Such places do not exist. You are playing an unkind trick on me."

"I promise I speak the truth and, if you are interested, then I would take you there. If you are not, then it is no fault of mine that you choose to miss out on the offer."

The boy turned his head and shouted up at a large rock, behind which two more children, of about the same age, were waiting. Their heads popped up and they drifted down shyly toward them.

"David says he knows where we can go to get food and shelter in exchange for a little work," he said, breaking into peals of laughter.

The two newcomers looked at him keenly. The boy started laughing too, but the girl stared at David with unwavering eyes.

"I have never known David to tell an untruth," she said, maintaining eye contact. "He does not shy away from my stare like one who lies would."

"Gather up some of the others and I will tell you more about the place that is being made ready for you. There is no reason for anybody to be afraid. I am here alone and you all know me."

The two boys disappeared behind some rocks, leaving the girl alone with David.

"This place really exists?"

"It does and it is being looked after by two people who will be familiar to you all."

"Who?"

"Jeremiah and the former Roman soldier, who now goes by the name of Arte. He was once a great leader of men, but now he puts his efforts into helping others. I myself have been helping with the preparations also."

More children began to appear, about twelve in all. They were filthy dirty and looked incredibly thin. Forming a rough circle around David, they sat down on the grass.

The oldest, however, a boy of about thirteen years old, remained standing and confronted David.

"Joshua has told us of the things you have said, and I ask why you have come here with such stories?"

"They are not stories. Once I had nothing, like you, but now I have food every day and clothes to wear. I sleep on a soft bed with a roof over my head – I have a home! I have been asked to offer you the same thing and all you have to do is give a fair day's work in return."

"Who has given you this food and shelter?"

David proceded to explain about Jeremiah and Arte as he had done with the girl.

"How can you trust a Roman soldier? Even as we sit here, they hunt us so that they might sell us into slavery!" he announced, indignantly

"Arte has given up his life as a soldier and is a good man who serves others. He helps provide food for the lepers in the caves. Michael knows him too and can vouch for his honesty, as do I."

"How close is this place to the lepers? He could spread the disease to us if he was not careful."

"He provides them with food but keeps a safe distance. Simon, the fisherman, would also speak for Arte. They would like to come and talk with you, along with the two men you stoned the other day."

"Why, what is their interest?"

"They are the ones who thought up the idea in the first place, and they have very worked hard to make this happen. They, along with the villagers, have laboured tirelessly to help create a safe place for you."

"Will you stay with us today, David?"

"I cannot. I am to take back your answer to them as soon as possible."

"It would do no harm to talk to them, but we will watch their approach from the village, and if anybody else follows then we will not meet them, and they will not be able to find us."

David continued negotiating until he managed to agree a time and place that met with the group's satisfaction. He understood the choice of venue, which was on a narrow clifftop path, a few miles along from the village. From its position, any others approaching along the beach or across the meadow land would easily be spotted from a long way off.

He returned to the village with the news that a meeting had been arranged for the following day, and all of them looked forward to it eagerly.

The meeting was led by Simon, whose gentle voice seemed able to allay any fears and mistrusts. Despite this, there were still those who would not take up the offer straight away. Jeremiah and Matt kept their comments to a minimum, unless asked something directly, and even then, they focussed mainly on such things as the type of shelter they were offering and the kind of work that would be needed in exchange.

In total, fourteen children agreed to come and view the caves for themselves, on the condition that no one else came along, other than the adults present. Simon gave them his word and the journey started almost immediately.

For those who chose not to go, a promise was made to accept any of them, at any time, if they felt the need for food and shelter. David told them as they walked away that there were a greater number of children left in the hills than who travelled with them now. Matt assured him that one day in the near future they would hear of how good life was at the caves and want to join.

When they reached their destination, the internal and external walls of the caves had been finished, and Arte proudly showed them around. He pointed out that none of the spaces had doors, reinforcing to them that they had a right to come and go as they pleased.

Their first meal, a hearty fish stew, was eaten with gusto and several had second and even third helpings. As night fell, each little group went inside the cave to a space they had selected earlier, and lay down on the beds of hay and straw. They were all asleep inside a quarter of an hour and Arte went round each hearth placing fresh wood on the fires that lit the spaces with a warm and cosy glow.

Miracles Do Happen

The children unintentionally awoke late the next morning, their unaccustomed comfort relaxing their bodies and minds into a long, deep slumber. Jeremiah, Arte, James and David had already been up for some time and prepared a light meal from last night's leftovers. Each child was given breakfast as soon as they appeared from their bed and were sitting around the communal fire, chatting shyly. They didn't seem to know what to do with themselves in this place of unexpected comfort.

Michael, the young boy who had helped with tasks for Arte when he was up in the hills, greeted Arte.

"Shalom! It is good to see you again."

"Shalom Michael! It pleases me that you have come here."

"If I am to stay here, then I need to know about the tasks that I would be expected to do to pay for my bed and my food."

"That depends on what you think you can offer the group that would benefit them the most. David works at cutting and shaping timber to make boats, but help is also needed gathering fuel for the fires, tending the goats, growing plants and many other jobs. You're free to choose the way in which you help and whichever task you undertake will be as valued the same as any of the others."

"It would please me to work with the nets that catch the

fish. I knew somebody that did this once and he taught me the skills as a very small boy."

"This would be a great help to the community, especially as the nets we have at the moment are old and fragile. I doubt they will last many more seasons. If you are serious about this, then we would be happy to exchange food and shelter for your services."

"I am. When can I start on this?"

"After everybody has been in the sea to wash the filth of their bodies and I have had the chance to clean your robes!"

"Why is this necessary?"

"Cleanliness is next to godliness, and the community we are building here is to be a very clean one," laughed James, as the boy wrinkled his nose in disgust at the thought of bathing in the sea.

One by one, all the children were encouraged to bathe in the sea and Arte and Jeremiah scrubbed each of the robes they removed. Some of the clothing was in such a threadbare condition as to be beyond any further use, but as they had no replacements, they could not throw anything away just yet. One of the girls told the group that she had skills in repairing clothes and Jeremiah made a mental note for her to visit Martha who was an excellent seamstress and who also knew how to weave new cloth.

Just before the sun disappeared below the horizon, every child was clean, fed and had a job that would benefit the community.

Simon, who had ventured away from the camp earlier in the day, made a sudden reappearance. He called Arte and Matt to him and wandered along the beach in the direction of the leper community.

"I have something to show you, Arte, something that will change your life forever but will also bring you and Jeremiah the direction, motivation and peace of mind that you have lacked for so long. It is a gift from the Rabbi for both of you and a release of the suffering of the others for whom you have also assumed responsibility to care. Matt, James, you are invited to witness this, because of the compassion and courage you showed when you stood alongside the lepers with Arte."

"It is getting dark Simon. Perhaps we should have brought some torches?"

"There will be torches enough when we reach the caves. The Rabbi was greatly moved when he heard of how the two villages had stood either side of those afflicted with leprosy when the soldiers threatened to kill them. He noted the way they had put their defence of the lepers above any concern to themselves. He observed that none showed any fear of catching the disease, and he said this was what his Father wanted everyone to be like. He was moved enough to pay them a visit at their caves, too."

They continued their journey until, suddenly, they were met at the cave entrance by two women, covered fully in robes that concealed their affliction.

"You are Arte – the man who was once a soldier and is now a fisherman; the man who has promised to take care of us, despite our illness. And you," she gestured towards Matt, "are the one who stood alongside me when we confronted the soldiers."

"I am the one you speak of, and this is James. Please tell me your name so that I may know to whom I am speaking."

"I am Ruth and this is my daughter, Mary."

"I am happy to meet you, Ruth, and you too, Mary. Shalom!"

"We were visited by the Rabbi today, Arte, and he talked about our life here in the caves. Then he prayed to God that he might ease our suffering. After he had finished praying, we were all, for just a fleeting moment, consumed with a fire that did not burn us, and when it had passed, the Rabbi asked us to remove the robes from our faces. Of course, we refused at first, having no wish to pass on our condition to him, but he encouraged us further, until Mary did as he requested. I will ask her to remove her hood now for you to see what has occurred."

Mary turned her back to them and removed the hood, to reveal raven-black hair falling to the small of her back. Then, as she slowly turned to face them again, Arte prepared himself for the horror that he knew befell all leprosy victims. Her dark brown eyes met his, and he felt compelled to gaze deeply into them. Her blink broke the gaze and he looked at the rest of her face. She truly was one of the most beautiful women he had ever seen, comparable to his own wife back in Rome. Then he realised what Ruth was trying to tell him.

"There is no trace of the disease!" he said in disbelief, and reached out to examine her hands, gently turning them over in his own.

Ruth removed her own hood and, although she was obviously older than her daughter, it was clear where Mary got her beauty from.

"The Rabbi has cured you?" asked Arte, in wonder.

"God, indeed, answered his prayers and cured us, Arte."

"I was cured too."

"And me."

"And me." A succession of voices echoed around the cave as, one by one, the group who had gathered there unnoticed by Arte, removed their hoods, revealing their unblemished faces.

"It truly is a miracle," said Arte, and he couldn't prevent a tear from falling down his cheek.

"The Rabbi left us with an instruction... more a request, really. Most of us, here, are women, but there are a few men too. We are to follow the guidance you give us and form a new community. The community we build must include the homeless children, and the concerns of your friend, Jeremiah, over the children needing a woman's care will be attended to by us. He said the task was huge but that Arte and Jeremiah are the right men for the job, and he is sure that the community will prosper. The three shoreline communities along this stretch of beach are to be united by the way of life the Rabbi instructs, and each will depend on the others at times of difficulty and hardship. Are you ready to lead us,

Arte – you and Jeremiah?"

"I give you my pledge now that I will gladly do as the Rabbi has instructed. Your needs will receive the best attention I can offer and if there are things I cannot do myself, then I shall seek the help of others so that our community will grow and flourish."

"Thank you, Arte. You are as the Rabbi told us."

"I would like to invite you all to my caves tonight. Will you come?"

"We would, but this might alarm the children who are newcomers themselves."

"Perhaps, then, just you and Mary? The others can see the truth in what I have to tell them."

"We would be honoured to come with you and the rest of us can follow once the children have settled in."

The darkness was all but absolute as they walked along the shoreline towards home, but a warm glow emitting from the caves, announced their presence under the towering cliffs.

Jeremiah walked down to meet them, having seen their torches. Arte told his friend about the Rabbi and everything that had occurred at the lepers' cave that day, and about the pledge he had made to his give his help in creating a new community. He was instantly smitten by Mary's beauty and found it hard to stop himself from staring at her.

Despite the miraculous nature of the Rabbi's work and the general sense of excitement, both Matt and James retired early, feeling unusually tired for this particular hour. Jeremiah made as if to call them back so that they could share the magic of a small celebration between those who had made all this happen, but Simon restrained him gently.

"Let them sleep, for they have played their part well in all that has come to pass, and rest is the least that is owed to them."

"Why don't you both discuss your ideas and thoughts for this place with Ruth and Mary, for I know there are plenty of them? A woman's perspective is often overshadowed by that of men and yet they have much more to contribute than is ever given credit. Besides, these two women have been looking after their own community for several years, just as you strive to do now. Their experiences will be invaluable in the days to come, as will the wisdom of what they have learned during their time as leaders."

"I am certainly interested in how they have survived for so long with the disease and while having to be more or less self-sufficient. I want to hear their stories."

"There is no time like the present then, Jeremiah, for the morning will be dominated by the needs of the children."

Simon left the four of them to talk by the fire and wandered down to the beach to a quieter spot where he knelt to pray. He asked for nothing personal, but prayed for everyone in the caves and thanked God for the generosity He had shown in curing the lepers. Finally, he thanked Him for sending the Rabbi.

Friendships were formed that night between the two men and women that would last their entire lifetime, and the weight of leadership was spread equally between them, to a point where each felt challenged but not over-burdened.

Matt and James slept on, oblivious to all of it.

Surprises

The dawn that following morning was breathtakingly beautiful, with braids of pinks, yellows and crimsons streaking across the sky, as if in competition to see which could reach the farthest. The wind had dropped to just a light breeze – perfect for a day's fishing. Matt and James awoke early and went for an early morning dip in the sea. Refreshed and revitalised they returned to the cave and realised there were two extra people busying themselves at the camp fire. Simon was there too, adding some wood as he looked up and saw them approaching.

"I trust you had a peaceful night's sleep?" he enquired, smiling in his usual peaceful manner.

"Actually, I slept very well, and am feeling really alive this morning," Matt answered.

"Me too – it must be all this fresh air," added James.

"Or maybe it is the result of all the good things you have done lately. When you feel good inside, everything else appears good, too. It is the peace and ease that God gives us for following His ways. Mary and Ruth stayed here last night to meet the children. They have pledged their help in building a new community that reaches far beyond just these children."

Matt said his greetings and sat at the hearth, waiting for Simon to add more, but he said nothing.

"Surely you are not going to make that statement, and then leave it without further explanation?"

Simon smiled easily again. "For now, I am! But after the morning meal is done, I would like you to come with me on a journey. It is a long journey so take whatever you need to make yourselves comfortable."

"How mysterious of you!" exclaimed Matt, feeling irritated at being kept in the dark.

"Rest assured, all will be revealed as we travel."

There was a real buzz around the camp as the children awoke and started the first day of real purpose they could remember. Each child couldn't help but smile as they began their new life, attacking their tasks with enthusiasm. James and Matt stood with Jeremiah and Arte, watching. All of them sensed at that moment that everything was right, and that this was the birth of something wonderful.

"You know, there should be a celebration to mark the things that have happened, something fitting which would include the two shore communities," suggested Matt earnestly.

"We were discussing this while you slept last night, and it will indeed happen very soon," answered Jeremiah.

Simon beckoned Matt and James to him, saying that they would be leaving shortly. A short while later, as they left the caves, they looked back upon the scene, trying to imagine what it would be like in a year's time.

"Time for you to tell us where we're going, Simon," urged James, as they reached the top of the cliff path and started across the easier grassland meadows.

"I thought you might like to see the Rabbi at his place of work."

"I was wondering if we'd ever get the chance to meet him. It seems that everyone else has, except us," commented James.

"The Rabbi moves from place to place, spreading the word of God. He is not always where you want him to be, although, if you truly listen, his words remain in your heart despite his absence."

"How much further do we need to go? I know there's still a lot of work to do back at the community."

"I am sure that your absence will not matter quite as much, now that there is a greater number of people to share the work."

The talk ceased and the three travelled in relaxed silence, their route gaining altitude all the time. James and Matt quickly realised that they were travelling back along the route where they had first entered this land. Catching each other's eyes, they exchanged a knowing look, although neither said anything.

They walked for about an hour, getting closer and closer to their arrival point, before coming upon a massive gathering of people, sitting patiently and quietly, obviously waiting for something to happen. Simon indicated for them to stop and sit, but they were still some distance away.

"Who are all these people Simon? And what is this place?" asked James.

"They are the Rabbi's congregation, and this place is where he works. He goes wherever people gather to teach about the word of God."

"I wouldn't recognise the Rabbi even if I were standing right in front of him, since I've never met him. Is he here yet, Simon?" asked Matt, scrutinising the crowd.

"He will be here shortly; it is what everyone is waiting for. You will recognise him, Matthew, simply by the aura that seems to shroud him."

Sure enough, after a few minutes, the low vocal humming emanating from the crowd increased as a man strode serenely towards its centre. Simon was right; there was an extraordinarily profound aura about him. The Rabbi began to address the multitude but from where they were, they could not quite make out his voice.

"I need to go to Him, for He has need of my service," stated Simon, even though no such request had reached Matt's or James' ears. "Stay here a while and witness the work of the Rabbi, and when you have seen enough, leave. Continue in the direction we were going, and know that the Lord walks with you wherever you go."

"Continue where?" James asked him.

"I do not know – it is simply the instruction the Rabbi asked me to give you."

Simon bade them 'Shalom' and walked down the hill towards the Rabbi, before anything else could be said. Matt made as if to stand up but James touched his arm and told him to wait. His eyes were shining with an excitement that made Matt want to question him, but James spoke first.

"I want to see this, and you need to as well. I'm having such a rush of ideas, maybe even realisation. But if I'm right, then things are suddenly going to make a lot more sense to us both. I think I know what's going to happen next!"

Picking up a stick, he traced something into a patch of dry dust. Matt leaned forward in an effort to see what his friend had drawn, but James concealed it with his foot.

"I can't make out what he's saying, James – we need to get closer."

"We can't, Matt. Trust me on this – it wouldn't be right."

"What do you mean?"

"All you need to do is watch and then you'll understand."

They watched Simon leave the Rabbi's side and greet a young man a little way off. The youth gave him a basket and Simon returned to the Rabbi. Opening the basket, he took out five loaves and two fishes, showing the Rabbi, who turned his eyes upwards. From their position, it looked like he was saying a prayer. Then he broke the loaves into small pieces, giving some to Simon and one or two other men close to him, who in turn started to share it out amongst the masses. The boys watched in wonder at what they were witnessing, before James broke Matt's concentration.

"You know what this is, Matt, don't you?"

"I can't believe what I am seeing, but yes!"

"It's time for us to leave – we have to go."

"I'd like to stay a little longer, see some more."

"We've seen enough; it would be wrong to stay."

"Why?

"I'll explain as we go," promised James.

The boys stood up and James turned away from the scene, starting up the hill again. Matt turned to follow and, as he took the first step, he noticed the marks James had made in the dust – it simply said '5000'. Initially, neither boy seemed to want to break the silence that had befallen them. Listening to the gentle rhythm of their steps, they were both engrossed in their own thoughts. But at the top of the hill, James stopped, turning back to the scene below. They both stared down at the now tiny figures below. They could just make out the Rabbi and Simon standing together, and they appeared to be looking up at them. Each raised a hand toward them and waved, with Matt and James responding in kind. After a brief pause as if to take one final look, possibly to embed the moment in their memory forever, they set off again, heading back towards the waterfall, and home, although neither had verbally acknowledged that this was their destination.

It was another hour before they reached it, and Matt finally broke the silence. His thoughts tumbled out all at once and his face was flushed with emotion.

"James, we can't go back yet – we *need* to talk about this, about what's been happening, about who I think we've been. We need to do it now, before we get lost into our real selves and while we're still older than we really are."

"You're right, Matt, we do, but I only have some of the answers."

"I have some too."

"You start then," encouraged James, knowing that his impetuously natured best friend would, anyway.

"Well, I think we've just witnessed one of the miracles from the Bible, and I don't think it was the only one. Now I know that the Rabbi was really Jesus, then the great storm we had at sea was the one that Jesus also calmed in the Bible. Simon said that the Rabbi was on his boat with him. We just saw the miracle from a different perspective. Then there was the healing of the lepers. I know we didn't see it happen, but there are countless tales in the Bible about Jesus healing the sick."

"So far, I agree with everything you've said. But have you had any thoughts about the people we've been for the past few weeks?"

"I'm still getting to grips with the things I've just said – I haven't thought that far, yet!"

"I think we've been disciples in this adventure. Think about it for a moment – Matthew and James! I don't know anything much about James, the disciple, but I know that Matthew was a former tax collector and, as such, was probably hated as they were often quite corrupt. It explains why you received such a hostile greeting when we first arrived. We misheard Simon when he spoke about a 'pilot'. I think he really said 'Pilate' as in Pontius Pilate! Lastly, of course, there's Simon. I reckon he is Simon Peter, the one usually just referred to as Peter!"

"If all of this is true, and I do believe it is, why did we become disciples? They're supposed to be the holiest of people. What did we do that they couldn't have done better?"

"I can't answer that, for sure, but I have an idea that could be on the right track or, possibly, completely wrong!"

"What is it, James?"

"Well, as twenty-first century people, we have different ways of doing things, different ways of thinking; different ways of talking. We're just *different*! I don't think that disciples would have acted as we did. They wouldn't have used physical tactics in the same way as we used our rugby skills. They wouldn't have thought of an orphanage which is probably a much more modern concept."

"Right or wrong, I like the way you put it, James. But we learned something else here, too. Something really important that we need to consider in future adventures."

"What's that?"

"We could get hurt, possibly even die, if we're not careful. Just because we're able to travel through time, it doesn't make us invincible. Asina could have done more to you than he did, and that was bad enough. But what if he had gone further?"

"It's not like you to deliberate like this, Matt. Normally, you're much more decisive."

"You're my best friend, James, we've known each other for a long time, since we were tiny. We do everything together and we always stand side by side. I want to make sure that we continue like that too."

"You're totally right, and we're going to continue that way but maybe we need to think things through a bit more before we act, especially if we separate during an adventure," James replied, and gently patted his friend on the back.

"I have another question. What do you think happens to the real people whose bodies we 'take over'?"

"I really couldn't say, but one thing we do know is that they don't 'swap places' with us. They don't become us when we become them, because we've already found that time stands still in our time when we go back. I'm beginning to think that they don't go anywhere, that they're still in this body, but sort of hibernating or something while we're here. We know that we don't always talk as we do usually; we're more mature. We also have other skills and abilities that we don't have in our own time. In Sherwood we were thatchers and blacksmiths. At Loch Ness, we were tour-guide operators on that boat. Here we're fishermen. There must be something of the real people still inside these bodies."

"That sort of makes sense to me too, and for now, I think I quite like the idea of it."

"One last question, James. Why did you want to leave when we saw Jesus about to feed the five thousand?"

"We were seeing something that I didn't think we should see. It's in the past."

"We've seen other things from the past."

"I know, Matt, but this was different. It's not easy to explain, but it's about faith. Everybody in our time who believes in God and the Bible, does so because of faith. You and I are now exceptions. We've *seen* Jesus with our own eyes! It's easy to believe in something when you've seen it, but not so easy when there's no proof."

"Did you believe in God, before you actually saw Jesus?"

"I think so, sort of. I like the idea of something wonderful being responsible for creating life. I like the idea of God and the peace that his words seem to give people. How 'bout you?"

"I think I've avoided answering that question, so far, because when I do think about it, I never seem to be able to make up my mind!"

"Perhaps we're too young to make up our minds yet, 'cause we still have so much to learn and experience. When I think about how the people at the village were content with so little – I wonder if that's a key thing. Having less allows you to appreciate something more.

"Do you realise that we have answers to questions that have been asked for generations?"

"That's true, but I also have questions that I don't yet have answers for. It could be that the mysteries from this place will be revealed much later, as we experience other new adventures in different places and times."

There was a brief silence, a pause for reflection before Matt said, "Lets go home James," and led the way up the rocks toward the waterfall.

It's kind of nice to know that wherever we go, we're not alone," James added, with a wry smile. "It's very reassuring."

Matt simply nodded in reply and stepped into the cascading torrent of water that separated them from their home, their time – and also from their next thrilling adventure.

Also by C. S. Clifford

Walking with the Hood – ISBN 9780993195730 - 2014/2016

Already thinking ahead to the next rugby season, James and Matt decide to spend their summer holidays in training to improve their fitness. On only the second day, however, their swim in the local river leads them to a waterfall whose cavernous depths take them out into another time and place.

Here they meet strange folk – strange yet very familiar folk they know only from books and films. Could they really be in Sherwood Forest talking with the legendary Robin Hood and his faithful band of brothers?

What's more, could two boys from the twenty-first century really help Robin, Will, Little John and the others take on the might of the infamous Sheriff of Nottingham and his brutal cousin, Guy of Gisborne? They don't know – but one thing's for sure: this will be a summer like no other!

Walking with Nessie – ISBN 9780993195709 - 2015

Having discovered the waterfall cavern earlier that summer, Matt and James couldn't wait to see where the mysterious portal would take them next.

They didn't have to wait long to find out...

Walking out into the breathtaking landscape of the Scottish Highlands, they discover that they haven't travelled very far back in time at all. It's the late 1960s, and in a small village just outside Inverness, international Nessie hunters have arrived!

All seems fine at first, but appearances can be deceptive. The boys soon learn that the visitors' sinister plans could put Nessie's life in danger - as well as their own.

C.S. Clifford has always been passionate about stories and storytelling. As a child he earned pocket money singing at weddings in the church choir; the proceeds of which were spent in the local bookshop.

He has taught in primary schools for the past ten years and was inspired to start writing through the constant requests of the children he teaches. He lives in Kent where, when not writing or teaching, he enjoys carpentry and both sea and freshwater angling.

Walking with the Fishermen is his third book.

www.csclifford.co.uk